She was pr ...

Very pregnant.

And when she looked up at him, her blue eyes were once again filled with the threat of tears.

"Maybe you could drop me at a motel? And maybe I could borrow enough money to pay for the night? I promise I'll pay you back. If you'll give me your name and address I swear you'll get every penny back." Her voice held a ring of desperation.

"I can't do that," Lucas said. "You're obviously in trouble. Tell me what's happened. Tell me your name."

Her lower lip began to tremble and her eyes filled with tears. "I can't." The two words were a mere whisper. "I can't tell you because I don't know. I don't know who I am."

CARLA CASSIDY

PREGNESIA

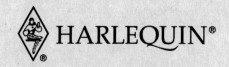

TORONTO • NEW YORK • LONDON
AMSTERDAM • PARIS • SYDNEY • HAMBURG
STOCKHOLM • ATHENS • TOKYO • MILAN • MADRID
PRAGUE • WARSAW • BUDAPEST • AUCKLAND

Recycling programs
for this product may
not exist in your area.

ISBN-13: 978-0-373-69413-6

PREGNESIA

Copyright © 2009 by Carla Bracale

www.eHarlequin.com

Printed in U.S.A.

ABOUT THE AUTHOR

Carla Cassidy is an award-winning author who has written more than fifty books for Harlequin Books. In 1995, she won Best Silhouette Romance from *Romantic Times BOOKreviews* for *Anything for Danny*. In 1998, she also won a Career Achievement Award for Best Innovative Series.

Carla believes the only thing better than curling up with a good book to read is sitting down at the computer with a good story to write. She's looking forward to writing many more books and bringing hours of pleasure to readers.

Books by Carla Cassidy

Don't miss any of our special offers. Write to us at the following address for information on our newest releases.

Harlequin Reader Service
U.S.: 3010 Walden Ave., P.O. Box 1325, Buffalo, NY 14269
Canadian: P.O. Box 609, Fort Erie, Ont. L2A 5X3

CAST OF CHARACTERS

Lucas Washington—Former navy SEAL and confirmed loner.

Jane Doe—What horror was her amnesia hiding and who was the father of her unborn baby?

Micah Stone—Lucas's business partner who would do anything to help his friend.

Charles Blankenship—Had it been a simple case of road rage or was Charles's involvement with Jane more ominous?

Robert Montgomery—Loving brother-in-law who wants "Jane" back where she belongs.

Church of Enlightenment—What did the strange church have to do with Jane's amnesia?

Chapter One

Lucas Washington stared at the darkened house
across the way from where he stood on a quiet residential Kansas City street. Although everything was
silent and it appeared the occupants of the house
were sleeping, Lucas knew this was the most dangerous time in the job he had to do.

He was about to repossess the two-year-old Buick
in the driveway, and he didn't know if there might
be a crazy man with a rifle in one of those darkened
windows ready to protest the repossession.

Lucas didn't believe in favors, giving them or
getting them. Still, it was repaying a favor that had
him standing on the street on a cold November night
at two in the morning. Repossessions were usually
done in the middle of the night when hopefully the
deadbeat was sleeping and there was less of a chance
of a confrontation.

As the third partner of Recovery Inc., it wasn't
unusual for Lucas to be repossessing some kind of

vehicle. But the business dealt in big-ticket items, speedboats and airplanes and such, and they often ventured into dangerous territories to get back whatever was necessary.

A two-year-old Buick wasn't their usual kind of job, but when Bob of Big Bob's Used Car Sales had called and asked Lucas to repossess the car, Lucas had reluctantly agreed.

Big Bob had given Lucas's sister a heck of a deal on her car and had overlooked the fact that Loretta's credit wasn't exactly stellar.

Besides, business had been slow lately and Lucas had been out of sorts. Maybe it had something to do with the fact that in the last four months his partners had both found love and suddenly had a life that didn't include him.

He scowled and pulled his collar up against the cold night air, then reached into his pocket and grabbed the key that Bob had provided him. All he wanted to do was get this car to Big Bob's, then go back home to his apartment.

According to Bob, who had financed the deal, the man who'd driven it off the lot hadn't made a single payment in four months. Bob's phone calls to try to work something out had gone unreturned, and so he'd called Lucas.

"No pay, no play." Lucas muttered. He hoped there wouldn't be any drama, that Mr. Deadbeat would wake up in the morning and wonder what in the hell had happened to his ride.

He approached cautiously, checking the windows of the house a final time then heading across the street. He crouched behind the back fender and listened, but heard nothing to cause him alarm.

Pulling the key from his pocket, he edged around to the driver's side and tried the handle. It was unlocked. Sweet. Mr. Deadbeat had made it remarkably easy.

He opened the door, slid into the seat and breathed a sigh of relief. He put the key into the ignition, cranked the engine and yelped as a hand fell on his shoulder.

He whirled around, expecting Mr. Deadbeat with a gun. Instead he found himself staring into the biggest, bluest eyes he'd ever seen. Female eyes. They belonged to a blonde who looked as if she'd just gotten the hell beat out of her.

A nasty gash decorated one side of her forehead. It had bled down her face and onto her white blouse.

"Please, if you're stealing the car, just let me out now." Her voice was thin and reedy and her face was pasty white.

"I'm not stealing the car, I'm repossessing it. What are you doing back there?" As he asked the question he backed out of the driveway.

He wasn't about to sit and talk with a bloody woman in the backseat with the engine idling when Mr. Deadbeat might come outside.

He pulled out onto the street and headed in the direction of Big Bob's. He glanced in the rearview mirror and saw her slumped in the corner, a perplexed frown on her pretty face.

"What are you doing in the car? Is it yours?" he asked. What in the heck was going on? "What happened to your head? Did somebody beat you up?" The questions snapped out of him. He didn't like surprises, and a banged-up woman in the back of the car was definitely a surprise.

He also didn't like the fact that she wasn't talking, wasn't offering any explanation for her presence. He frowned and shot her another glance in the rearview mirror. Maybe she was seriously hurt.

"Do you need to go to a hospital?" he asked more gently.

"No!" The word shot out of her like the report of a gun. "No, please." Her eyes were shiny with tears. "Just drop me off someplace. I'll be fine."

A domestic issue? he wondered. Maybe she was afraid that if she went to the hospital, whoever hurt her would find her. He tightened his hands on the steering wheel. There was nothing he despised more than a guy who abused women.

"Look, if your husband or boyfriend hurt you, then you really should go to the police."

"Please, no police, no hospital. Wherever you're going I'll just get out there and everything will be fine."

"What's your name?"

His question was met with silence and once again he looked at her in the rearview mirror. She met his gaze, then quickly looked out the side window. "My name isn't important," she finally said.

"Is this your car? Your husband's car?"

"No, I don't know who it belongs to. It was the only one on the block that wasn't locked and I was cold. I was just going to sit in it for a little while and try to warm up before leaving."

Something definitely wasn't ringing true. She wasn't telling him her name or what had happened to her. He'd get the car to Big Bob's, then figure out what he was going to do with the young woman.

What he'd like to do was drive her straight to a police station or to a hospital, but he'd heard the absolute panic in her voice when he'd mentioned either option.

His quick, easy favor for Bob was turning into something much more complex, and that was the last thing Lucas wanted or needed.

He breathed a sigh of relief as the car lot came into view. He told himself that he wasn't a part of whatever drama the woman in the backseat had going on and yet there was no way he could just dump her at Big Bob's.

She was obviously in some sort of trouble. He needed to get a closer look at the gash on her forehead to see if she needed medical attention.

He turned into the lot and pulled through a gate that led to a secured area. He'd park the car, drop the keys into a lockbox, then close a gate that would make it impossible for Mr. Deadbeat to retrieve the vehicle using the key he still had in his possession.

He glanced to the backseat where the woman lay, her eyes closed and looking as pale as the winter moon. He pulled through the gate, parked the car and cut the engine. Only then did she open her eyes and stare out the window as if terrified of what might happen next.

"I won't hurt you," he said softly. "I need to leave this car here, but mine's parked close by and I'll be glad to take you wherever you need to go."

He opened his car door and got out, then opened the back door. She stepped out of the backseat with obvious reluctance, and as she did, he gasped in stunned surprise.

She was pregnant.

Very pregnant.

The idea that somebody had beat up a pregnant woman caused a wealth of unexpected protectiveness to surge up inside him.

She was only about five-two, dwarfed by Lucas's six feet. And when she looked up at him, her blue eyes were once again filled with the threat of tears.

"Maybe you could drop me at a motel? And maybe I could borrow enough money to pay for the night? I promise I'll pay you back. If you'll give me your name and address I swear you'll get every penny back." Her voice held a ring of desperation and promise.

"I can't do that," he said. "You're obviously in trouble. Tell me what's happened. Tell me your name."

Her lower lip began to tremble and her eyes filled

with tears. "I can't." The two words were a mere whisper.

She drew a deep, tremulous breath and leaned back against the Buick. "I can't tell you because I don't know." She raised a hand to her forehead and winced. "I don't know who I am."

Lucas narrowed his eyes and stared at her, wondering if she was for real. She could be lying through her straight, white teeth.

She shivered and he knew he had to make up his mind quickly. She was coatless and pregnant, and somebody needed to clean that wound on her head. He'd do what he could to help her tonight, but in the morning she'd have to be on her way.

She might not be telling him the truth about having amnesia, but there was no way he could just abandon her in her present condition.

"Look, my apartment isn't far from here and my sister lives down the hall from me. She's a nurse. You need somebody to look at that cut on your forehead. Why don't I take you there and we'll figure out what to do with you after that?"

She eyed him warily and placed her hands on her protruding belly. "I don't know you," she finally said.

"My name is Lucas. Lucas Washington." He raked a hand through his long, shaggy hair. "I don't know about you, but I'm freezing and just want to get home. You're obviously in trouble, and if what you told me is true, then you need to trust somebody. It might as well be me."

"You'll take me to your sister's?" she asked. Lucas nodded. "And she's a nurse?"

"That's right."

"Okay," she agreed, although there was still more than a little wariness in her voice.

As Lucas walked to his car with her following just behind him he told himself he'd see her safely through what was left of this night, but tomorrow she had to go. He wasn't about to get any more involved in whatever drama she had going on in her life.

COULD SHE TRUST HIM? She didn't know. He seemed all right even if he did look like what she'd assume a car thief might look like. At least he wasn't a car thief. She just wasn't sure what else he might be.

As she got into the passenger side of his sports car, she shot him a surreptitious glance. His black hair hung nearly to his shoulders and framed a face that was lean and slightly dangerous looking. The black leather jacket he wore stretched across broad shoulders and his dark jeans hugged slender hips and long legs.

On some level she found him intensely attractive, but could she trust him? Her head pounded with nauseating intensity. But the pain couldn't touch the frantic terror that clawed inside her.

Why didn't she know her name? How had she gotten hurt? Why couldn't she remember anything? She was pregnant and she didn't even know if she was married or not. She wasn't wearing a ring, but that didn't necessarily mean anything.

"You all right?" Lucas asked as he turned into the parking lot of an apartment complex.

At least he hadn't driven her to some field where nobody would hear her scream. "I guess," she replied. "To be honest, I'm terrified."

He pulled into a parking space, then turned to look at her, his eyes dark and enigmatic. "You don't have to be terrified of me. I promise I won't hurt you."

"I think that might be what all serial killers say just before they murder somebody," she replied.

A rumble of deep laughter escaped him as he turned off the engine. "I guess I never thought about that before."

He got out of the car and she did the same, comforted by the fact that if he did try to hurt her and she screamed, surely somebody in one of the apartments would hear her.

She had to trust somebody. She had no money, no identification and a headache that threatened to topple her to her knees. The night was cold, and she was beyond exhaustion. Even if she didn't care about herself, she cared about the baby she carried.

Surely after she slept she'd remember who she was and what had happened to her. All she needed was a couple of hours of rest and everything would become clear again.

She followed him into the building and down a long hallway. Not a sound came from any of the doors they passed. It was almost three in the morning and the building held the silence of a tomb.

"This is my place," he said softly as they passed apartment 104. "My sister's place is at the end of the hall."

When they reached the apartment numbered 108, Lucas knocked softly on the door. There was no reply and he rapped harder.

"I feel terrible," she whispered. "It's the middle of the night and you're waking her up."

"Loretta won't mind," he replied, and knocked once again.

The door cracked open and a pair of sleepy dark eyes that looked remarkably like Lucas's peered out. "Lucas, what are you doing here at this hour of the night?" The door closed again and there was the sound of a chain being removed and then the door opened all the way.

Loretta Washington was as petite as her brother was broad. She had the same rich, black hair and dark eyes, and those eyes widened as they saw her. She opened the door wide enough to allow them entry and then belted her short blue robe more tightly around her waist.

"What's going on?" she asked.

"Jane here has a problem," Lucas said.

Jane? As in Jane Doe. She supposed for now the name would serve her as well as any. "I'm sorry to bother you in the middle of the night," she said.

"Nonsense, come into the kitchen where I can get a look at that head wound." Loretta had a calm efficiency about her that put Jane somewhat at ease.

She allowed herself to be led through a tidy living room and into a small kitchen with a round wooden table. "Sit," Loretta instructed, pointing to one of the chairs at the table.

Jane complied and fought an overwhelming desire to weep with relief. She sensed safety here, at least for the moment. Lucas sat in the chair across from her and eyed her with the same wariness that she'd used on him. Looking into his dark eyes, that sense of safety was more tenuous.

"What happened?" Loretta asked as she got a first-aid kit from under her kitchen sink.

"She doesn't know," Lucas said, but his tone indicated that he didn't quite believe her.

"I wasn't talking to you," Loretta exclaimed. She got a damp cloth and began to wipe the side of Jane's face. Jane closed her eyes against the gentle touch. "What happened, honey?"

"I don't know." She winced as Loretta began to clean the cut. "All I remember is running and running. Then I was tired and cold, so I crawled into the car where your brother found me."

"She says she has some kind of amnesia or something. She doesn't know her name," Lucas said, and once again his voice was laced with a touch of suspicious disbelief. "For the time being I'm calling her Jane."

Jane met his gaze. Those dark eyes of his seemed to look inside her soul, but there was nothing there for him to see.

"You don't know your name?" Loretta asked gently. "Do you know what day it is?"

"November second or third." Jane knew she must be right because Loretta nodded with encouragement. Loretta asked her several more questions, about the year and who was the president.

"I know all that," Jane said. "I just don't know who I am and what's happened to me." Again fear bubbled up inside her and she fought against it, refusing to show either of them just how terrified she really was.

As Loretta checked Jane's blood pressure and pulse, Lucas continued to watch her with hooded eyes that gave nothing away.

"Well, the good news is your vitals are all normal and you don't need stitches on your forehead," Loretta said. "But you really need to go to the hospital to be checked out for other head injuries."

Panic swelled in Jane's chest. She wasn't sure why, but she felt that if she went to a hospital or to the police, she'd only be putting herself in more danger. "No, I'm sure I'll be fine if I can just get some rest." She looked at Lucas once again. "Maybe you could take me to that motel we talked about earlier?"

"Nonsense," Loretta exclaimed. "It's almost morning now. There's no reason for you to go anywhere. I have a spare room where you'll be perfectly comfortable for the night and we'll sort out everything else in the morning."

"Oh, I couldn't impose anymore," Jane said, offering a weak protest.

"Don't bother arguing with her," Lucas said. "Loretta might be small, but she's as stubborn as the day is long."

Loretta cuffed him on the back of the head and gave him an affectionate grin. "Why don't you get out of here and let us women get to bed?"

"Walk me to the door?" he said to his sister.

Loretta nodded, and as she followed Lucas out of the kitchen, Jane slumped forward and cradled her belly in her arms as she felt the baby move around inside her.

At the moment the only thing she was certain of was that she loved the baby she carried. She had no idea who the father was, or what her relationship might be with that man, but it didn't matter. She had a feeling she'd loved the baby from the moment of conception.

What would she have done if Lucas Washington hadn't stumbled upon her? Where would she be at this moment? Still in the backseat of that car, slowly freezing half to death? And what would she have done in the morning when she had to leave the car?

She shivered and again a low pulse of fear filled her. It was more than the fear of not knowing her name. It was some innate knowledge that she was in danger. And the most frightening part was not knowing who might be after her and why.

Chapter Two

Lucas sat at his kitchen table and watched the morning sun peek over the horizon. He'd only slept for a couple of hours, but felt rested. He'd never needed much sleep. Not sleeping too soundly or too long had been a survival mechanism learned in his youth, with his father's explosive temper that could erupt anytime day or night.

He tightened his fingers around his coffee mug as he thought of those nights of terror. If it hadn't been for his younger sister, he wasn't sure he'd have survived his childhood.

Initially he'd worried about leaving a stranger with Loretta for the night, but he'd realized a very pregnant woman with a head wound didn't pose much risk. Besides, Loretta was tougher than she looked.

Jane.

She'd haunted what little sleep he'd gotten. Once Loretta had cleaned the blood off her face, Lucas had gotten his first real look at her. She was stunning, with her heart-shaped face and big blue eyes. Her complexion was smooth and her skin had looked soft and supple.

He'd been surprised by the tiny kick of pure male lust in the pit of his stomach. He was thirty-three years old and rarely felt that particular feeling. And he'd certainly never felt it for a pregnant woman suffering from amnesia.

He consciously willed himself not to get interested in any woman. He had his work and his sister and that's all he'd ever really needed.

Getting up from the table, he stretched with his arms overhead. He needed a shower. By the time he was done his sister would be awake and he could check in on Loretta and her patient.

As he stood beneath a hot spray of water he thought about the mysterious Jane. He suspected she might be lying. Even though there had been genuine fear in those gorgeous eyes of hers, he wasn't convinced that her amnesia was real.

What he thought was that she'd probably had a fight with her boyfriend or husband and had concocted the amnesia story to buy her a little time. As long as she didn't go to the police or to the hospital, the man in question couldn't find her or go to jail on domestic abuse issues.

Surely by this morning she would have "remembered" her name and found forgiveness in her heart for the guy who banged her up. It happened all the time. It was a story Lucas knew intimately.

He dressed in his customary jeans and pulled on a ribbed, long-sleeved navy shirt, then returned to the kitchen for another cup of coffee before heading to his sister's apartment.

He needed to call one of his partners and let them know he wouldn't be in to the office until later in the afternoon. He needed to figure out where to bring Jane and wasn't sure exactly what to expect.

Lucas and two of his ex–navy SEAL buddies had started Recovery Inc. when they'd gotten out of the service. The company dealt in recovery of both items and people in sticky situations and had been successful beyond their wildest dreams.

Despite the financial rewards, Lucas lived a simple life. He used most of his money to help pay Loretta's student loans and was determined to help her pay for medical school next spring. Her dream had always been to be a doctor, and Lucas wanted to make sure she achieved that dream.

He pulled his cell phone from his pocket and punched in the number for Micah Stone, one of his partners and his best friend.

Micah answered on the first ring. "Hey, partner, what's up?"

"I just wanted to let you know that I won't be in this morning. I've got some things to take care of, but I should be there sometime this afternoon."

"That makes two of us. It looks like Troy will have to hold down the fort by himself," Micah replied.

"I'm being fitted for a tux this morning. Have you been fitted yet?"

Micah's wedding was less than a month away and Lucas was serving as his best man. "Not yet. I'll try to get in before the end of the week."

"If you don't, then you know Caylee will be chewing on your backside. And trust me when I tell you she has very sharp teeth."

Lucas laughed. Caylee was Micah's fiancée. She was definitely a spitfire, but Lucas had never seen his friend so happy.

"Then I guess I'll see you sometime this afternoon," Lucas replied, and the two men hung up. Lucas was glad Micah hadn't asked him why he'd be late. He wasn't sure why, but he wasn't eager to share the night's events and his mysterious Jane with anyone.

If she'd taken advantage of their kindness, as he suspected, then he sure didn't want his partners to know he'd been taken for a fool.

He finished his coffee and checked the clock. Just after seven. Loretta would be up by now and he was eager to see what Jane had miraculously remembered this morning.

When he reached Loretta's apartment door he rapped lightly and his sister answered almost immediately. She was dressed for the day in blue-flowered scrubs and held a cup of coffee in her hand.

"I've been expecting you," she said, and motioned him to the kitchen. "My houseguest is still asleep."

"Did you talk to her after I left last night?" Lucas leaned against the counter.

"A little, but not much. She was exhausted and I figured the best thing for her was a good night's sleep. I take it you don't believe her story."

Lucas raised an eyebrow. "Do you?"

Loretta sat at the table. "I don't know. I do think she had a trauma of some kind and she seemed genuinely afraid and confused. She looks to be around eight months pregnant. If some man whacked her upside the head, he should be hung by his manly parts for the rest of her life."

Lucas grinned. "Ah, Loretta, tell me how you really feel." Love for his sister surged up inside him. Loretta was six years younger than him. With both their parents dead and the history they shared, the two siblings were particularly close.

"What I feel is that you need to put your overactive cynicism aside when you talk to her. She may not have amnesia, but she's obviously in trouble." Loretta drained her coffee cup and got up from the table. "I've got to get to work."

Lucas walked with her to the front door where she turned to look at him once again. "Feed her something, Lucas. And if she needs to stay here a couple more days, it's fine with me." She reached up and kissed Lucas on the cheek, then left.

Lucas returned to the kitchen, poured himself a cup of coffee and then sat at the table. He wasn't surprised by his sister's generous offer to a stranger. Loretta made a habit of helping people.

Sometimes it amazed him how his sister had survived the dysfunction of their past with such a goodness of spirit, such a pure, sweet soul. Too bad he couldn't say the same about himself.

He had his cup halfway to his mouth when Jane appeared in the doorway. She was clad in a white nightgown that stretched taut across her breasts and her belly. Her blond, curly hair was tousled, and it was obvious by the widening of her eyes that she'd expected to find Loretta, not Lucas, in the kitchen.

"Oh!" She instantly hunched her shoulders and crossed one arm over her breasts. Her lower lip trembled and her eyes looked as if she'd been crying. Once again Lucas felt a strange surge of protectiveness. "I'll just…I'll be right back." She darted out of the kitchen and back down the hallway.

It was only then that Lucas realized he'd been holding his breath. He took a sip of his coffee and tried to forget the vision of her, so soft and feminine, and so utterly vulnerable.

She returned moments later, this time clad in the jeans and the dirty, bloodstained white blouse she'd worn the night before.

"Doesn't Loretta have something you can wear?" he asked.

"Your sister is tiny." She placed a hand on her stomach. "And right now I'm not. She didn't have anything big enough to fit my stomach."

"Sit down and I'll get you a cup of coffee," he said.

He got up as she sat. He poured her a cup of coffee and carried it to the table, where he set it before her.

"How are you feeling this morning?" he asked.

To Lucas's horror, she burst into tears. "I thought everything would be all right this morning," she said between sobs. "I thought I'd wake up and I'd know who I was and what happened, but I don't know any more now than I did last night."

The sobs were painful to watch. Lucas grabbed a handful of napkins and handed them to her. She was either the greatest actress on the face of the earth or she was telling the truth.

She cried so hard he got worried about her, about the baby. He pulled up a chair next to her and awkwardly patted her back. "Don't cry," he said. "We'll sort this out, but you've got to stop crying. It can't be good for the baby."

That seemed to penetrate into her head, because the sobs wore down to sniffles, and finally ceased altogether. She wiped her cheeks, and when she looked at him once again, there was desperation in her eyes.

"I'm so afraid," she said. "I don't know what's going to happen to me."

"For now, nothing is going to happen," Lucas replied. "You're safe here. Loretta told me to tell you that you're welcome to stay for a couple of days until you feel better."

Tears welled up in her eyes once again. "I can't believe how kind you're being to me."

He wanted to tell her that it wasn't him, that his

sister was the kind one. He was the cynical one who still didn't know whether to believe her or not.

But for the moment he decided to give her the benefit of the doubt. If she was lying, then sooner or later he would know. If she was telling the truth, then he sure as hell didn't want to be responsible for tossing a pregnant woman out on the streets all alone with no money and no memory.

"Are you hungry?" he asked.

"Starving. I can't remember the last time I ate." A half-hysterical spurt of laughter burst out of her.

"Scrambled eggs okay?" he asked as he got up from the table.

"Fine. But please, you don't have to wait on me. If you'll just show me where things are, I can do for myself." She started to get up, but he waved her back down.

"I'll take care of it, just sit tight." He got the eggs from the refrigerator and set to work making breakfast.

As he worked she stared out the window, tiny frown lines dancing across her forehead. Again he was struck by her prettiness. She wasn't screamingly drop-dead gorgeous, but rather she had a quiet, simmering beauty. He frowned and whipped the eggs more forcefully than necessary.

The last thing he needed was to be attracted to her. She obviously had a man in her life. And in any case Lucas didn't do relationships.

She continued to stare out the window as if lost

in thought while he fixed the eggs and popped in toast. Then once it was all done he placed the food on two plates, one for her and one for himself.

"Lucas?" She turned to look at him, her blue eyes troubled. "I know this sounds crazy, but I have a terrible feeling that I'm in real danger."

He set the plates on the table with a sinking sensation in the pit of his stomach. This was growing more complicated by the minute. And there was nothing Lucas hated more than complication.

JANE STARED AT HIM and tried not to notice that his dark hair had a gleaming shine to it that made it look silky soft and that he smelled like soap and shaving cream and a hint of a clean cologne. "You don't believe me, do you?"

Since the moment she'd told him that she didn't know who she was, that she had no idea what had happened to her, she'd sensed his suspicious disbelief. And she wasn't sure why it was so important to her that he accept what she was telling him.

"I don't know what I believe," he finally replied. "I think it's possible you had a fight with your boyfriend or husband or whatever, and you need a safe place to hide out until things cool off and the two of you can kiss and make up."

She reached up and touched her forehead with a frown. "I can't imagine wanting to kiss and make up with anyone who did this to me."

He picked up his fork. "He'll buy you flowers or candy and swear he'll never touch you again and you'll end up going back and things will be great until the next time he loses his temper." His voice held a harshness in tone.

"I wouldn't be involved with a man like that," she exclaimed.

He raised a dark eyebrow. "How do you know?"

She felt the warmth of a blush on her cheeks. "I might not know who I am, but I know what I'd tolerate, and I'd never stay with a man who put his hands on me."

She felt a swell of tears burning at her eyes and bit them back. She'd cried herself to sleep the night before and had awakened and cried some more. She was tired of crying. "Maybe nobody hit me. Maybe I just fell and hit my head on something," she said.

"I don't think so," he replied. "Do you have bruised knees? Scraped-up palms? Anything that might indicate you'd fallen?"

"No."

"That scrape on your head doesn't look like it's the result of a fall. It looks like you were hit with something." He leaned forward and she realized his dark eyes had tiny shards of silver in them. "You know, if you're just scared and need a place to hang out for a couple of days, it's all right to tell me. You don't have to make up any stories."

"I'm not making anything up. I don't know what

to do to make you believe me. I don't know what to say to make you understand that I'm not lying."

Those dark eyes of his studied her intently. "Eat your eggs and toast before they get cold."

They ate for a few minutes without speaking, until she couldn't stand the tense silence another minute longer. "Your sister seems really nice," she said.

He nodded. "She's a sucker for people in need."

"And you're not?"

The corners of his lips turned up in a humorless smile. "I'm not a sucker for anyone or anything."

"I know your sister is a nurse, but I'm not sure exactly what it is you do."

"I own a company, Recovery Inc., with two of my friends. We were all Navy SEALs together, and when we got out of the service we opened the business."

"And you repossess cars?"

He frowned, as if the question irritated him. "Last night was not our normal kind of job. I did that as a favor for the owner of the car dealership."

"So, what is your normal kind of job?" she asked. It was a welcome relief to be wondering about him instead of wondering about herself.

"We recover items and return them to the people they belong to. But it's really not important what I do. What's important is what we're going to do about you."

"I should probably go. I'm really not your problem." She tried to ignore the terror that coursed through her at the thought of having to leave, of not knowing where she would go.

"If I let you leave under these conditions, Loretta will have my head," he replied. He stood and grabbed their plates from the table and carried them to the sink. "Our first order of business today is to get you a few things from the store. You need a change of clothing and some personal items if you're going to stay here for a couple of days."

She felt terrible. She didn't want to take advantage of either Loretta or Lucas. But no matter how much she wanted to claim back her own life, she didn't know where to begin.

"I can't believe this," she said more to herself than to him. Once again she directed her gaze out the window where the sun hid beneath a blanket of low gray clouds. She felt as if the sun was her memory, hiding someplace inside her and refusing to come out into the light.

She looked at him once again and cradled her stomach with her arms. "If it were just me, I'd leave. I'd never take advantage of your kindness."

He leaned against the counter, those dark eyes of his impossible to read. "I'll go to my place and get you a T-shirt and a jacket, and we'll head to Wal-Mart to pick up what you need."

"Whatever you buy for me, I'll pay you back. I swear I will just as soon as I figure out who I am and where I belong." She frowned and tried to ignore the headache that had begun to pound across the top of her head. "Maybe as the day wears on, something will jiggle my memory."

She couldn't imagine going day after day with no memories, with no knowledge of something as simple as her own name.

"Maybe," he replied. He shoved off from the counter. "I'll just get that shirt and jacket. I'll be right back."

As he left the kitchen she leaned back in her chair and drew a deep breath. She raised a hand and touched the scab that had formed on her forehead.

What had happened to her? Why couldn't she remember? What if a couple of days passed and she still didn't know who she was, or where she belonged? What then? She couldn't just continue to stay here forever. She could take advantage of Loretta's kindness only so long.

She dropped her hand to her belly and rubbed with a caressing motion. She thought the baby was a boy. Of course she didn't remember anyone telling her that, had no concrete memory, it was just something she knew. Like she knew that she hated peanut butter and loved pizza.

Lucas returned with the large T-shirt and a down-filled navy ski jacket. She took the shirt and returned to the bedroom where she'd slept to put it on.

Her bloodstained blouse was probably ruined. She couldn't imagine any laundry detergent that would be able to wash away all traces of the blood.

Lucas's T-shirt hung across her slender shoulders

and pulled slightly across her belly, but wearing the clean cotton material that smelled faintly of fabric softener made her feel better.

She left the bedroom and found Lucas waiting for her on the sofa. He stood as she entered the room, his gaze sliding from the top of her head down to her belly.

Self-consciously she placed a hand on her stomach. "Your shirt isn't exactly made for two," she said. "I hope I don't stretch it too much."

"I'm not worried about it," he replied, and held out the coat to help her into it.

It easily wrapped around her and along with its warmth brought that scent of him, that pleasant fragrance of clean cologne and male. She found it oddly comforting.

"Ready?" he asked.

She nodded and together they left Loretta's apartment and walked out into the hallway. "Am I keeping you from a wife or a girlfriend?" she asked as they passed his apartment door.

"No, you aren't keeping me from anything or anyone," he replied.

"What about your job? Shouldn't you be at work?"

He flashed her a quick smile. It was the first smile she'd seen from him and it shot a flutter of warmth through her. "One of the perks of owning the company is getting to pick and choose when you decide to work."

She nodded and fell silent as they walked out into

the brisk November air and headed for his car. What kind of a woman was she to be carrying somebody else's baby and feel that burst of heat at the smile of a virtual stranger?

There had been a moment when his gaze had drifted over her that she'd wished her tummy was thin and shapely, that they'd met in the grocery store or at a restaurant and were together because of a mutual attraction.

Maybe she hadn't just lost her memory, maybe she'd lost her entire mind, she thought as she slid into his passenger seat.

Stress. It had to be stress that had her thinking such crazy thoughts. The only thing she knew she could count on, at least for the moment, was Lucas and his sister. Was it any wonder she would be attracted to him?

"If you don't recover your memory sometime today, then tomorrow I'll make some discreet inquiries about missing persons reports that have been filed in the last day or so," Lucas said as he started the car. "Surely somebody you know will get worried and report you missing."

"Unless nobody cares that I'm missing," she replied.

He shot her a quick look. "I would find that hard to believe."

She released a wry laugh. "I find this entire situation hard to believe."

"Let's play a little game. I'll ask you some questions and you give me the first answer that pops into your head."

"Okay," she agreed as he pulled out of the apartment parking lot.

"What's your favorite television show?"

"The Closer," she replied without any real thought.

He nodded. "Good. And what was the last movie you went to see?"

"I don't go to the movie theater very often." She tried not to think about the tiny nuggets of information the answers revealed about herself, afraid that the nuggets would stop coming.

"What's your favorite restaurant here in the city?"

"That's easy, Café Italian on Maple Street." A buzz of excitement went off inside her. "Maybe they'll know me in there. Maybe they can tell us who I am."

"I know the place. It isn't far from where I found you last night in the car. Maybe we'll go there for lunch and see what we can find out."

Jane's excitement grew. It was possible that by lunchtime she'd know who she was; she'd at least know her name. Surely that would make it easier for her to find out what had happened to her.

"It's a place to start," he said, invading her thoughts. He pulled into the Wal-Mart parking lot and found a space near the front door. At this time of the morning the store didn't look too busy.

They got out of the car and had taken only a

couple of steps toward the door when a voice inside her head thundered.

Don't let them find you.

The words seemed to come from some separate entity inside her brain and they screamed with an alarm that froze her in her tracks.

Instinctively she reached out and grabbed Lucas's hand as fear charged through her. He curled his fingers with hers as he looked at her with concern. "Are you all right?" he asked. "Is it the baby?"

Two thoughts raced through her mind. The first was that she liked the way his big, strong hand felt around hers, and the second was that the voice she'd thought she'd heard in her head had probably been nothing more than a response to the drama of her situation.

She suddenly felt foolish. She unfurled her fingers from his and gave a small laugh. "No, it's not the baby. I guess I just had a case of nerves."

He dropped his hand to his side and studied her intently. "There's nothing to be nervous about. The only thing you have to worry about is being overwhelmed by all the choices."

She forced a smile. "That never happens with women," she said.

Once again they began to walk to the door. Surely the words that had thundered in her head meant nothing, she told herself. But what worried her was they hadn't sounded like nothing. They had sounded like a warning...but a warning of what?

Chapter Three

Once again Lucas found himself doubting the veracity of her amnesia story. Something had happened in the parking lot. He thought she might have thought of something or remembered something that she apparently didn't want to tell him.

She didn't trust him. How could he help her if she didn't trust him?

Lucas pushed the cart with one hand, took Jane by her elbow and guided her down an aisle. When he'd seen her in his T-shirt he'd realized how tiny she was despite her pregnancy. The baby weight was all up front like a ball in her belly, but everywhere else she was slender.

"If you'll just get me a blouse and a toothbrush, that should be enough," she said as they walked through the linen section toward the back of the store.

Lucas didn't know a lot about women, but there was no way he believed she could make do for a day or two with just a new blouse and the jeans she had on.

When they reached the maternity clothes, she headed directly to a clearance rack. Apparently she meant to spend as little of his money as possible.

As she thumbed through the discounted items, he spied a blue cotton long-sleeved blouse exactly the color of her eyes and plucked it from the rack. He threw it into the basket, then added an oversized blue and white sweater.

Although she hadn't mentioned it, she probably needed some underwear, too. He certainly didn't want to completely outfit a woman who might return to a husband or a boyfriend before nightfall. She had a life somewhere, with clothes and shoes and everything else necessary. Still, he didn't want her to do without the bare necessities while she was with him for a day or two.

She returned to where he stood with the cart, carrying an ugly gray T-shirt that had probably been the cheapest on the rack.

"I don't think so," he said. She looked at him in surprise. "If I'm going to be looking at you for the next day or two, I don't want you wearing something ugly."

"But it's only five dollars," she protested.

"There's a reason it's so cheap." He took it from her and hung it on a nearby rack. "What about that pink shirt there?" He pointed to a pastel T-shirt that said Baby on Board. "With another pair of slacks, you should be all right with the other things I grabbed," he said. He averted his gaze from her.

"Then we'll head to the underclothes department and you can get what you need."

She grabbed him by the arm and when he looked at her, those beautiful blue eyes of hers were once again misty with tears. "I can only hope that the father of this baby is half the man you are, Lucas."

"Don't make me into some kind of a hero," he replied with a definite edge in his voice. "I'm just doing what anyone would do under the circumstances."

As they left the maternity section and headed to the undergarments department, he wanted to tell her that he was the last person she should look at with such soft, appealing eyes, with that hint of hero worship that made him feel too warm inside his own skin.

As she picked out a package of panties, he stood at the end of the aisle and waited for her. An old woman stood at the other end of the aisle and appeared to be looking at Jane. When she saw Lucas she offered a sweet smile, then moved on to another aisle.

Jane returned to the cart and threw in her choices. Her cheeks were slightly pink as she looked at him. "I hope I'm a wealthy woman because I'm going to owe you a bunch of money."

"Don't be silly," he replied. He pointed to the nightgowns. "You need to pick out one of those," he said.

"Oh no, that's all right. Loretta gave me one to wear," she replied.

Lucas frowned, remembering when she'd stepped into the kitchen in his sister's nightgown.

"That one can't be comfortable. I saw how it pulled across your stomach. Just pick out one that will fit you comfortably."

As she moved to the rack to look at the items, he tried to forget that vision of her. That nightgown of Loretta's hadn't just pulled taut across her belly, but across her breasts, as well. Her hair had been all tousled and she'd looked achingly soft and feminine.

For just an instant as he'd held that coffee cup frozen halfway to his mouth, he'd wondered what it would be like to wake up with a woman like Jane next to him. When half-asleep, would he rub the swell of her belly and dream of the future of the baby she carried?

Jeez, what was wrong with him? He'd never thought about babies before. The last thing he'd ever wanted to be was a husband and a father. He simply wasn't cut out for either role. Jane felt just a little dangerous to him. She made him think of things he'd never thought of before.

She picked a pale pink nightgown and added it to the growing number of items in the shopping cart. He then pointed the cart in the direction of the toiletries section. She walked beside him and paused a moment to rub her lower back.

"Sorry," she said, and smiled. "Junior must be stretched out right along my spine."

Her smile torched a wave of heat through him. It was the first true smile he'd seen from her and it did amazing things to her already-lovely face. Even the scab across her forehead couldn't detract from her attractiveness.

Suddenly, he was irritated. All he wanted to do was solve the mystery of his Ms. Jane Doe and get her on her way and out of his life.

He noticed the old woman who'd been in the underwear section now at the end of the aisle where Jane stood in front of the hair care items. Once again when she saw him looking at her she smiled. She dug a cell phone out of her purse and then disappeared around the corner.

It was easier focusing on a little white-haired woman than watching Jane. He'd been too long without a woman. That was the problem. It had been months since he'd been out with anyone.

His last date had been with a friend of his partner Troy's girlfriend, Bree. Miranda had flown in from California for a weekend visit and Lucas had taken her out. She'd been perfect for him, very hot and very temporary. He frowned in irritation as he realized Jane got to him in a way Miranda hadn't. There was a softness about Jane, a sweetness in her smile, a fragile light in her eyes that pulled up a protectiveness in him he'd never felt for anyone except his sister.

"I think that's everything I should need." Jane pulled him from his thoughts as she added a hairbrush, a toothbrush and a bottle of citrus-scented shampoo to the cart.

"Then let's get out of here," Lucas said. He blew a sigh of relief as they headed for the cashier lines.

Maybe if he took her to Café Italian for an early lunch, somebody at the restaurant would recognize her and the mystery would be solved.

They fell into line behind a woman who looked as if she'd bought half the store. Jane covered his hand with hers on the handle of the cart. Her hand was warm on his skin as she looked up at him. "I can't thank you enough," she said. "I couldn't face wearing that bloody blouse all day today."

"We'll run back to Loretta's so you can change clothes, then head to the restaurant to see if anybody there knows your name."

He breathed a sigh of relief as she pulled her hand from his. "Even if somebody just knows my first name, surely hearing that will remind me of who I am."

He heard the thrum of desperation in her voice. It must be horrifying not to know even the most simple thing about yourself—your name. Until this moment he hadn't really realized that if she was telling the truth about her amnesia, then she must be absolutely terrified.

All he'd been thinking about was getting her gone as soon as possible, but he didn't want her to go unless she had her memory back.

Finally it was their turn to be checked out. As Lucas placed the items on the counter he noticed that Jane winced and rubbed her lower back.

"You want to go ahead to the car?" he asked. Maybe if she got off her feet her back would feel better.

"Are you sure you wouldn't mind?"

He held out the keys as the cashier told him his total. "Go on, I'll be out in two minutes."

She smiled gratefully and took the keys from him as he pulled out his wallet to pay the cashier. As she headed toward the exit, he put the bags of his purchases back in the cart.

As he pushed out of the exit door, he saw a van pull up. The back doors opened and two men began grappling with Jane, obviously trying to get her into the back of the van.

"Hey!" he yelled. His heart smashed into his ribs as he abandoned the cart and took off running toward them.

At that moment Jane released a scream that raised the hairs on the back of his neck and drew the attention of everyone in the parking lot. Another shopper, a burly man, began to run toward the van, as well.

Jane screamed again as she struggled to get free. The two men suddenly released her and jumped into the back of the van, which took off with a squeal of tires.

The burly man and Lucas reached Jane at the same time. She launched herself at Lucas, wrapping her arms around his neck and hanging on tight.

"Are you all right?" he asked urgently. "Did they hurt you?"

She shook her head and buried her face against his chest. Despite the fact that she wore his big, down-filled coat, he could feel the trembling of her body against him.

The big man looked at Lucas and pulled a cell phone from his pocket. "Want me to call 911?"

"No!" Jane lifted her head and looked first at the man, then at Lucas. "No, please. Let's just go home. But thank you for your help."

The man shrugged and put his cell phone back in his pocket, then headed toward the store entrance.

Another shopper, a young woman, pushed Lucas's cart to where he and Jane stood. "You aren't safe anywhere these days," she said with a worried frown on her face.

With Jane still clinging to him, Lucas pushed the basket to the side of his car. She pulled his keys from her pocket, unlocked the door and helped her into the passenger side.

He threw the bags into the backseat, then walked around to the driver door. It had all happened so damn fast. He hadn't even gotten a license plate number on the van. All he'd seen was a small symbol of some kind on the back window.

There was no way he believed that this had just been a random act of violence. Those men had been after her. As he slid in behind the steering wheel he turned to look at her. His heart still beat a rapid tattoo of alarm.

"If you have any memories in your head, if you're holding anything back, you'd better spill it now," he said as he stabbed the key into the ignition. "Otherwise we'd better figure out who you are and why in the hell those men just tried to kidnap you."

Jane stared at him as the yawning horror of what had just happened filled her with an icy chill of terror. When the van had pulled up in front of her, she'd thought nothing about it. Then the back doors had swung open and the two men had rushed her.

"I swear I don't know anything. I don't know who those men were or what they wanted with me." Her heart still beat with the frantic rhythm of fear.

A knot of tension throbbed in Lucas's lean jaw as he pulled out of the parking lot and onto the road.

She continued to look at him, needing the mere sight of him to ground her, to somehow chase away the panic that still clawed at her insides.

"I don't suppose you recognized those men?" he asked.

She shook her head. "I don't think I've ever seen them before."

"Did they say anything to you?"

"No, not a word. They just grabbed me and tried to get me into the back of the van." She shuddered as she relived the moment when they'd grabbed her arms, when they'd begun to force her toward the vehicle.

Lucas didn't say another word as they drove back to the apartment. As he drove he checked the rearview mirror constantly and she realized he was watching to see if they'd been followed.

He didn't sign up for this, Jane thought. *He didn't*

volunteer for whatever was going on in my life. But
the idea of not having him next to her terrified her.

When they reached the apartment he grabbed her
by the arm and walked her inside the building, his
gaze seeming to go in all directions at the same time.

"Why don't you go and take a shower and change
clothes," he said. "Then we'll head to that restaurant
and see if anyone there can identify you."

The idea of leaving the safety of the apartment
terrified her, but she knew she couldn't just stay here
and hope that her memories might magically return.
Maybe being in the familiar surroundings of the restaurant would jog something loose.

She brought the shopping bags into the bedroom
where she'd spent the night, then carried the clean
clothes and the other items into the bathroom for a
quick shower.

As she stood beneath the hot spray of water she
thought of the moments when the men had grabbed
her. She'd been so stunned that she'd been unable to
think, and had reacted only by fighting back. She'd
kicked and punched to get away, but they'd seemed
determined to get her into the back of the van.

Why? Who were those men?

Don't let them find you!

The words thundered in her brain and she leaned
against the porcelain wall as wave after wave of fear
swept through her.

Were those men the "them" that her brain had
screamed a warning about? What did they want with

her? Who was she? The questions pounded her as the hot water pelted her skin.

What kind of trouble was she in?

When she was finished showering, she dressed in the new clothes, the maternity jeans feeling crisp and clean against her skin and the blue blouse fitting her perfectly. She found Loretta's blow-dryer beneath the sink and dried her hair, then brushed her teeth and pronounced herself ready for what the rest of the day might bring.

She found Lucas seated at the kitchen table, doodling on a piece of paper. He looked up as she entered, and for an instant she saw the flash of something dark, something hot in his eyes.

She might not know her own name, but she knew desire when she saw it. It stunned her and at the same time sent a shock wave of excitement through her.

There was no question that she was attracted to him, that his lean, dark good looks made her heart beat just a tiny bit faster. But she'd attempted to shove away those crazy feelings. She was carrying somebody's baby, and for all she knew she was in a happy, committed relationship with another man.

"You look nice," he said.

She wrapped her arms around her stomach. "I look pregnant," she replied, as if somehow reminding herself and him of that fact.

A corner of his mouth curled up in a smile. "You can look pregnant and nice at the same time."

"Thank you," she said, aware of the flush that warmed her cheeks.

She sat at the table across from him. "What are you doing?"

"Unfortunately I didn't get a good look at the two men who were trying to grab you, and I didn't get the license plate of the van, but I did notice a sign in the back window."

"A sign? What did it say?"

"It didn't say anything. It was a symbol of some kind. I tried to draw it to see if maybe you'd seen it before." He shoved a piece of paper to her.

She stared down at what he'd drawn—a triangle with what looked like the all-seeing eye in the center. The sight of it shot a cold, stark terror through her. She gasped and pushed it back across the table to him.

He leaned forward and covered her hand with his. "Do you recognize it? What is it, Jane? What does it mean?"

"I don't know." She felt ill, as if the cold November air had brought icy snow into her veins. "All I know is that seeing it makes me feel sick. It makes me so afraid."

She turned her hand over and twined her fingers with his, needing the warmth of his hand to banish some of the chill. "What does it mean, Lucas? My God, what was going on in my life before I lost my memories?"

"I don't know. But those men definitely had

something in mind for you." The throb of that muscle was back in his jaw.

Reluctantly Jane pulled her hand away from his. Her heart thudded anxiously as she looked at the man who had taken her in. "Lucas, maybe you should just drop me off at a shelter or something." The words came reluctantly and with a thunderous pounding in her head. "I don't know what kind of danger I might bring to you and Loretta."

His eyes narrowed. "Danger has never scared me." He leaned back in the chair. "There's no way anyone can tie you to me. I'm not concerned about danger finding you here. And there's no way in hell I'm going to drop you off anywhere until we know what's going on. I don't think those men intended to take you someplace for a nice hot cup of tea."

A river of gratitude washed over her. It would have been so easy for him to abdicate all responsibility for her and toss her to the proverbial wolves.

She cradled her stomach as the baby moved inside her. "Junior is restless," she said.

"Maybe he's hungry." Lucas pushed back from the table and stood. "Come on, let's check out that Italian restaurant. Maybe over bread sticks we'll learn your real name."

They put their coats back on, then left Loretta's apartment. "We need to stop by my place before leaving," he said.

When they reached his door he unlocked it and gestured her inside. "I'll be right back," he said, and disappeared down the hallway while Jane looked around the living room with interest.

It somehow didn't surprise her that his living conditions were spartan and as impersonal as a motel room. He'd been completely at ease in Loretta's apartment. She had a feeling he spent most of his free time there.

There was only one photo in the room and it sat on top of the television in a silver frame. She walked over and picked it up. It was a picture of him and Loretta sitting on a park bench. He looked to be around fifteen and she was nine or ten. She leaned into him, smiling up at him as if he were the greatest thing since sliced bread, but his smile looked slightly forced.

She set the photo down as he returned to the living room. "You and Loretta have always been close?"

"It's always been her and me against the world," he replied.

"What about your parents? Are they still alive?"

"No, they're both dead. But even when they were alive, Loretta and I only had each other."

She wanted to ask him more about the dark shadow that had danced over his eyes when he'd mentioned his parents. But his terse tone and frown forbade her from asking anything else.

They left his apartment and walked back out into the cold, wintry air. She got into his passenger seat and watched as he walked around the front of the car to the driver side.

As he moved, his coat blew open to reveal that he

now wore a holster with a gun. Jane's mouth went dry. She'd known she was in trouble when those men had tried to grab her, but the sight of that gun suddenly shot it all home.

He was expecting more trouble. That's what the gun meant. She only hoped they both would survive whatever happened next.

Chapter Four

The Café Italian was a popular lunch place. They had a reasonably priced luncheon menu and promised fast service for those who only had an hour or so to eat before returning back to work.

Lucas and Jane were greeted at the door by a smiling, robust man who looked as if he'd been eating pasta and garlic bread for most of his life. "Two?" he asked as he grabbed a couple of menus.

Lucas nodded and they were led to a table in the back, where Lucas sat facing the door so he could see who was coming and going. Jane took off her oversize jacket and sat across from him. "Have you been working here long?" Lucas asked the man as he handed them their menus.

"Just started a couple of weeks ago," he replied. "Why?"

"Do you recognize me?" Jane asked.

Lucas heard the desperation in her voice and wondered how she was managing to hold it all together. Certainly after the scene at the store she had every right to fall apart, but she hadn't and she'd earned a grudging admiration from him.

"Should I recognize you?" the man asked as he studied her face carefully. "Are you somebody famous?"

"No, nothing like that," she replied. "I just…I'm having some memory problems and I remember being in here and hoped somebody would be able to tell me when."

"Sorry. I'm pretty good with faces, but I don't remember seeing yours before," he replied. "I'll ask the waitresses if any of them recognize you."

"Thanks, I'd appreciate it," she replied.

As he left their table, she looked at Lucas with a disheartening frown. "I thought I'd just walk in here and everything would come back to me."

"Do you remember anything?"

She leaned back in her chair and looked around. Lucas had known the blue blouse would match her eyes, but he hadn't thought about how it might make her skin look creamy and touchable. He hadn't considered that with the top buttons unfastened he'd get a hint of cleavage each time she bent forward.

"I don't remember anything specific, but this place feels familiar. I know for sure that I've been here before. I just don't know if it was a week ago, a year ago or five years ago." She puffed a sigh of obvious frustration. "What if I never remember who I am or why those men tried to grab me?"

"It's only been a day, Jane. Maybe you're trying too hard," he replied.

She smiled. "Having a couple of goons try to grab you in a parking lot tends to make you try hard." She sighed once again and opened her menu. "The eggplant is delicious here." Her gaze shot to his in stunned surprise. "How did I know that? Why can I remember eggplant when I can't remember my own name?"

She was getting more and more agitated with each minute that passed. Lucas frowned. "I think maybe after we eat we'll go back to my place and just relax for the rest of the afternoon. Stop reaching for it and maybe it will come."

"Maybe you're right," she agreed as she closed her menu.

With each minute Lucas spent with her, more questions whirled in his head. What did that symbol mean that he'd seen on the back of the van? Why had Jane reacted so viscerally to it? And why had those men tried to grab her? What could they possibly want from her? It sure as hell hadn't been a robbery attempt. She wasn't even carrying a purse.

If the cashier had taken one more minute in loading up his purchases, if he'd stopped to look at something on his way out of the store, then they would probably have succeeded in getting her into the back of the van. The thought chilled him to the bone.

His thoughts were interrupted by the arrival of the waitress to their table. Jane ordered the eggplant and he ordered lasagna. Then Jane asked the woman if she'd seen her in the restaurant before.

"You look kind of familiar," she said. "I'm sure you've been in here before, but I don't know your name or anything."

"We knew this was probably a long shot," Lucas said as the waitress left with their orders.

"I know. I just hoped that we'd at least get a first name." She tucked a strand of shiny hair behind her ear. "So, talk to me about something else, Lucas. Tell me more about yourself." She smiled. "The good thing about being with a woman who has amnesia is that the conversation gets to be all about you."

He laughed, finding her more than a little bit enchanting. "There isn't much to tell. I'm thirty-three years old, never been married, never intend to get married. I love my work, my sister and my partners and that's about it."

"Why don't you have any intention of marrying?" she asked.

"Because I'd probably be a crummy husband and an even crummier father." He was intimately familiar with bad relationships and bore the scars of horrible parenting. That's what he knew. By staying single, by never becoming a husband or a father, he would never run the risk of repeating the mistakes his parents made.

"I don't think you'd be crummy at either," she said. But she really knew nothing about him.

"I'm just better off alone." He shrugged, slightly

uncomfortable by the conversation. "I'm happy that way."

"I know it sounds crazy, especially given this little circumstance." She patted her tummy. "But I feel like I was alone before all this." Her cheeks flushed a becoming pink. "I don't know, maybe the man who got me pregnant decided he didn't want anything more to do with me or the baby." She picked up her water glass and took a sip, then continued. "It's just a crazy feeling I have."

"Maybe you feel that way because of the circumstances," he replied. "Maybe you have a loving husband somewhere waiting, worrying about you right now."

She looked down at her hands. She had slender fingers with neatly clipped nails and wore no polish. "I'm not wearing a ring. I'm not sure how to explain it, but I just know in my heart that I'm not married."

He didn't know what to think. Certainly just because she was pregnant he couldn't automatically assume that she was married. Maybe deep down inside he hoped she was. He hoped she had a loving man in her life who was worried sick about her, a man who loved her to distraction and couldn't wait for the birth of their baby.

Although he'd known her less than twenty-four hours, he wanted that for her. And maybe he needed to believe that in order to erect a barrier between them.

There was no question that he was attracted to her.

More attracted than he could remember being to a woman in a very long time.

As the waitress arrived to serve them, he tried not to think about that attraction. He told himself it was nothing more than the way she looked at him, as if he could fix her life, as if she trusted him to make things right. Loretta was the only other woman who had ever looked at him like that.

He was as temporary in her life as her amnesia and he hoped that within another twenty-four hours she'd have her memories back and be out of his life.

Lunch passed uneventfully. They chatted about the food and she asked him questions about his partners, Micah and Troy.

He told her about how Micah had found love with Caylee when he'd gone to a private island to retrieve an airplane. And Troy fell in love with a California paparazzi favorite, Brianna Waverly, while protecting her during a kidnapping.

Brianna now ran an animal shelter not far from the Recovery Inc. office, and Lucas had a feeling it wouldn't be long before they'd begin planning a wedding.

"When we get back home I'll check in with Troy and Micah and see if they can hunt down some information about that symbol I saw in the van window," he said.

Her face paled. "Seeing it gave me a terrible feeling," she said, her voice higher than usual with obvious stress.

"Maybe if we can figure out what it means, then we'll have a clue to your identity."

"So you do believe me? You don't think I'm faking?" Those blue eyes of hers held his gaze intently.

A man could drown in those blue depths, he thought. Maybe it was because she had no past, no baggage, that her eyes were so clear, so achingly blue.

"Yeah, I believe you." It was true. At some point after those men had tried to grab her at the store, he'd realized she wasn't pretending. He'd seen the stark terror on her face coupled with utter confusion. Nobody was that good an actress.

"I'm so glad," she replied. "It was important to me that you believe me."

"Why?"

She looked at him in surprise. "Because you're helping me. Because you and your sister have already gone above and beyond for me. I don't want you to think that I'm the kind of woman to lie and take advantage of you."

He might not think she was a woman who would take advantage of him, but he had a feeling she was definitely the kind of woman who could get him into trouble if he wasn't careful.

BY THE TIME THEY GOT BACK to Loretta's apartment Jane was exhausted. "Why don't you go lie down for a little while," Lucas suggested. "You look beat."

"I am," she agreed.

"While you're resting I'm going to call my

partners and see what they can find out about that symbol. I'm friendly with the chief of police, Wendall Kincaid. I'll give him a call and see if anyone has filed a missing persons report about a pregnant woman."

She frowned. "But you won't tell the police about me?" He hesitated and she took a step closer to him. "Lucas, I don't think I'm a criminal and I have no rational reason for my fear, but the idea of going to the police makes me as afraid as the sight of that symbol did. I know eventually if I don't remember who I am we'll probably have to go to the police. But please, not yet?"

"Don't worry," he assured her. "I'm not going to go against your wishes right now. I can ask Wendall some questions, and if he asks why I want to know, I can tell him that I have an issue I'm not ready to tell him about right now. He'll respect that. But if this amnesia continues, then you're right, we might have no choice but to go to the police. Go on, get some rest."

With a nod, she turned and walked down the hallway to the bedroom where she'd slept the night before. She couldn't imagine actually going to sleep, not with the questions whirling around in her head.

Once again she found herself wondering what might have happened to her if Lucas hadn't found her in the car. He was like a guardian angel come to her when she needed somebody.

But was it normal to feel a rivulet of heat when a guardian angel looked at you? Was it normal to wonder what his mouth might feel like pressed against your own?

Hormones, she thought as she stretched out on her back on the bed. Her hormones were definitely running amok and that was the only reason for her crazy physical attraction toward Lucas.

She rubbed her stomach as she felt the baby moving inside her. Who was the father? What had happened that had sent her out into the cold in the middle of the night with a head wound?

Maybe Lucas was right. Maybe she was trying too hard to remember, and her efforts were stifling the very memories she was trying so hard to retrieve.

She closed her eyes and consciously willed away all thoughts of the moment when the two men had grabbed her arms and tried to get her into the back of the van. She drew in deep breaths and tried to empty her mind of all thought.

Symbols. They were everywhere. The triangle with the eye inside it. The all-seeing eye. The all-knowing mind. Her heart crashed inside her chest as she ran down a long, dark hallway, needing to escape from it…from them.

Footsteps sounded behind her and she pressed her back into an alcove, praying they'd move on, that she wouldn't be found.

She breathed a sigh of relief as the sound of the footsteps faded away. Run! *Her brain screamed the command.* Get out!

Once again she began to move silently down the hallway, hoping she'd come to a door that would allow her to escape. She turned into another corridor and stopped, her blood cold as she saw him standing at the end.

Even though the hall was too dark for her to see his features, she knew who he was—the all-knowing mind.

SHE SCREAMED as hands gripped her by the shoulders and she opened her eyes to see Lucas. The dream fell away, but not the horror of it. She gasped as a sob escaped her lips.

"Hey, you're okay," he said as he sat on the edge of the bed. "You were just having a bad dream."

Cold. She was cold with terror and she didn't think twice about launching herself into his arms as another sob ripped out of her.

He stiffened as she pressed against him and hid her face in his chest. Then he did exactly what she needed; he folded his arms around her and held her.

In the warmth of the embrace, in the strength of his arms, any tears she'd been able to shed vanished. A dream. It had just been a dream. Or had it?

"You okay?" His voice was a rumble in her ear as she kept her head against his broad chest.

Although she found his embrace amazingly welcome, she knew she couldn't stay in his arms forever. Reluctantly she sat up and moved away from him.

"You want to talk about it?" he asked.

She wrapped her arms around her shoulders, the cold wind of fear finding her once again. "It was crazy. There were those symbols everywhere and I was in a dark hallway, trying to escape."

"Escape from what?" Lucas's dark eyes watched her intently.

She frowned, trying to make sense of the images that she'd dreamed. "I don't know. It didn't make sense. I just knew that I had to get away and then I turned a corner and there was a man standing at the end of the hall and I knew I couldn't get away." A shudder worked through her.

"Was it a dream or was it a memory?"

Jane held his gaze. It would be easy to get lost in those black-lashed dark eyes of his. At the moment she'd like nothing more than to get lost in him, to escape the uncertainty of the unknown, to feel safe and secure in his arms.

She shook herself. "I'm not sure. I don't know," she finally replied. "But if it was a memory, then what could it mean? I mean, why would I feel as if I was a prisoner trying to escape something awful?"

Lucas ran a hand through his hair. "I don't know. Maybe it was some kind of symbolism. Maybe what you were trying to escape was your amnesia."

"Maybe," she said grudgingly, although she wasn't sure what to believe. "How long was I asleep?"

He looked at his wristwatch. "About an hour or so."

He got up from the edge of the bed. "Look, I've

got some things to do. You should be fine here until Loretta gets home. She should be here by four."

She didn't want him to leave. The idea of being alone terrified her, but she swallowed the fear and nodded. "Please, take care of your business. I'll be fine." She offered him a smile that she hoped didn't look as forced as it felt.

"I'll check in with you later this evening." As he left the room, Jane felt an overwhelming need to tell him that she didn't want to be by herself, but she didn't.

She'd intruded into his life in a very big way and the very least she could do was not be a clinging vine to a man who owed her nothing just because she was overwhelmed with fear.

Fear. She slid her legs over the side of the bed and drew a deep breath. She had to get control of her fear. There were a million things she didn't know about herself, about her life, but she needed to focus on what she did know.

She and the baby were healthy, and at the moment she was in a safe place. Maybe after another good night's sleep her memory would return. Maybe during dinner tonight she'd have a sudden epiphany and all her memories would just come tumbling back.

Instead of feeling sorry for herself or afraid, maybe she needed to get her mind on something else. With this thought in mind she headed for the kitchen.

Maybe she could do something nice for Loretta

and cook dinner. Looking in the refrigerator, she spied a pound of thawed hamburger meat. Maybe a meat loaf, she thought.

Within minutes she'd gathered all the ingredients she needed to make the dish and set to work. Funny, she had a feeling she made a great meat loaf, and adding the appropriate amount of bread crumbs and seasonings came to her without thought.

She'd just popped it into the oven when she heard the sound of the front door open. "Hello?" Loretta called out.

"I'm in the kitchen," Jane replied. As Loretta came into the room, Jane felt a touch of shyness. She'd hardly spoken to the woman the night before and hadn't seen her that morning.

"You look much better than you did last night," Loretta said with a warm smile that instantly put Jane at ease.

"Maybe on the outside, but unfortunately nothing has changed on the inside," Jane replied.

"Still don't remember anything?" Loretta asked as she sat in one of the kitchen chairs and kicked off her blue clogs.

"Nothing. I hope you don't mind that I'm still here. I took the liberty of making a meat loaf for dinner."

"Mind? If you cook for me every night I might just think about marrying you," Loretta exclaimed with a laugh.

Jane relaxed and joined her at the table. "I don't

want to take advantage of your kindness. I'm hoping maybe after another good night's sleep things will become clear."

"Don't worry about taking advantage. What's important is that you give yourself some time to get your memory back. Where's my brother?"

"He said he needed to take care of some business and left about an hour ago. He said he'd check back in sometime this evening. He's been very kind to me."

Loretta smiled. "He can be a bit hard and crusty on the outside, but he's a good man." She frowned and looked as if she wanted to say something more, but instead she stood. "I'm going to go take a quick shower. I'll be back in a few minutes."

"If you don't mind, I'll go ahead and set the table."

"Mind? Knock yourself out," Loretta exclaimed, and then left the kitchen.

Jane found the appropriate plates and silverware and got the table prepared for the meal. She made a salad, opened a can of corn and got it warming on the stove top by the time Loretta had returned, now dressed in a pair of sweats and a T-shirt.

"Now, tell me about your day," she said as she put a kettle of water on the stove to boil for tea.

Jane told her about their trip to the store and the kidnapping attempt. As she related the story, that familiar cold fear seeped into her bones.

"Oh my God," Loretta exclaimed when she was finished. "You poor thing."

"Even that didn't jiggle loose any memories, but Lucas said he was going to have his partners do some research and see if they could find out what the symbol means."

"If you're in some kind of trouble, Lucas, Troy and Micah are the men to help you out. If there are answers to be found, they'll find them."

A half hour later as they ate, Loretta told Jane about Lucas's partners and the business that they owned. But what Jane wanted most of all was to learn more about Lucas.

"Your brother told me that when you two were growing up it was you and him against the world. You had a tough childhood?" she asked.

Loretta frowned thoughtfully. "Not so much me, but things were tough on Lucas. My father had anger issues and most of his rage was always directed at my brother." She shrugged. "He got through it. We both did. But it made us unusually close. Lucas was my hero when I was growing up, and throughout the years that's never changed."

"It must be nice to have somebody like that in your life," Jane said. "Somebody who will always be there for you, somebody you can depend on." A wistfulness filled her and again she couldn't help but wonder if she'd been looking for somebody like that in her life or if she'd already found him and just couldn't remember who he was.

"Yeah, the only thing nicer than having a brother like that would be having a husband like that,"

Loretta said with a laugh. "But there will be time for romance once I'm finished with medical school."

The rest of the meal they chatted about Loretta's desire to become a doctor and speculated on what Jane might do as a career. It didn't take long for them to get silly. Loretta thought Jane might be a Hollywood actress who had escaped the prying eyes of the paparazzi to have her baby in private. Of course the baby's father was a high-profile rock star who loved her to distraction, but was afraid marriage would hurt his image.

Jane offered the scenario that she'd been abducted by a space alien and impregnated and they'd erased her memories so she wouldn't bring back secrets of their planet.

The laughter felt wonderful and they were still giggling like high school best friends when Lucas walked in.

Instantly, Jane felt as if the kitchen shrank in size as he filled it with his dark energy, his bigger-than-life presence.

"Sounds like you two are having fun," he said as he grabbed a plate from the cabinet and sat at the table.

"We were just speculating on Jane's life," Loretta explained, her eyes still sparkling with merriment. "We've decided she's either a spy or a hooker going incognito."

Jane laughed again. "Your sister is a hoot."

Lucas filled his plate from the food still on the table. "Yeah, she's a regular comedian."

"What have you been doing?" Loretta asked.

"I had to go try on a tux for the wedding. Then I stopped at the office to catch up on things," he replied.

"Wedding?" Jane asked.

"My partner Micah is getting married in less than a month. I'm his best man. Good meat loaf," he said.

"You can thank Jane for dinner. She surprised me by fixing it. I told her if she cooks like this every night I might decide to keep her," Loretta said.

"You might have to keep her, at least for another day or two." He grabbed a piece of bread to add to his plate.

"I talked to Kincaid at the police station. There've been no reports of missing women filed in the past forty-eight hours."

Jane stared at him in dismay. She'd somehow hoped that a missing persons report would fill in some of the pieces.

She wasn't sure what bothered her more, the fact that strange men had tried to shove her into the back of a van or that apparently there was nobody in her life who had missed her over the past twenty-four hours.

Chapter Five

The crushed look on Jane's face touched a chord in Lucas's heart. "Maybe it's too early for anyone to have reported you missing," he said. "If you went missing not too many hours before I found you, then it's only been twenty-four hours now. Maybe tomorrow somebody will file a report."

"Maybe," she agreed. "Or maybe there was nobody in my life to file a report, nobody who misses me."

"I can't imagine that," Loretta said gently.

What must it be like to be missing from your life and believe that nobody cares? Lucas couldn't help but feel a chord of sympathy for her despite his desire to the contrary.

He listened and ate while the two women talked about babies and fashion, acting as if they'd known each other forever. The first time he heard Jane laugh, the sound shot a burst of warmth through him. She had a great, full-bodied laugh.

Who had she been before all this? Had she laughed often? Loved passionately? Did she like old movies or New Age music? Did she like quiet, intimate dinners or prefer the club scene? He frowned, irritated that he was even speculating on who she really was.

As Loretta got up to begin clearing the table, Jane rose, as well. But Loretta waved her back down. "No way. You cooked, so I do the cleanup. Just sit and relax."

Jane sat back down. She'd only been sitting a minute when a smile lit her face and she placed her hands on her tummy. "Junior is doing a happy dance." She smiled at Lucas. "Quick, give me your hand."

Without conscious thought he leaned forward and placed his hand on her belly.

Immediately he felt the undulating movement of life. A sense of awe filled him as he felt a flutter, then a sharper protrusion of an elbow or a foot. A baby, a little human life—amazing, he thought.

He jerked his hand away and sat back in his chair. He didn't want to think about babies or beautiful blondes who had smiles filled with sunshine. He refused to get emotionally caught up with the unborn baby and Jane, who would eventually remember her life and return to it.

"I've got to get home," he said, and stood, needing to escape the warmth of Jane's smile and the concern that she was all alone in the world, had somehow been all alone in the world even before she lost her memories.

"Tomorrow I want to take you to the office to meet with my partners. Micah is working to get us some information about that symbol and on the way we'll take a ride by the place where I found you. Maybe something will break loose in your head if we go back to that area."

"What time should I be ready?" Jane asked him.

"Let's say around nine?"

He walked over to his sister and kissed her on the cheek. "I'll see you later," he said.

He breathed a sigh of relief as he escaped the apartment and headed down the hallway to his own. He had no idea what it was about his "Jane Doe" that affected him so strongly.

Even throughout the last couple of hours when he hadn't been with her, his thoughts kept returning to her. What if the baby came? Who was going to take care of her and the newborn if she didn't have her memory back?

Dammit, he didn't want to feel responsible for her, and yet he did. And if he were completely honest with himself he would admit that despite the fact that she was pregnant, he was attracted to her. Never in a million years had he thought he'd find a pregnant woman sexy, but he found Jane extremely sexy.

He entered his apartment and checked his machine. No new messages. He hadn't expected any. His partners knew to get him on his cell phone and there wasn't anyone else who would want to call him. He sat on the sofa and for a moment the silence closed in around him.

The sound of Jane's laughter had found a place inside him that whispered of a loneliness he hadn't realized was there. Her warm laughter had momentarily chased it away.

What he needed was for her to wake up tomorrow and not only remember her name, but also have a family to support her, perhaps a husband who loved her.

What he really needed was a good night's sleep without thoughts of Jane intruding in his head. He grabbed a beer from the fridge and returned to the sofa, where he punched the remote to turn on the television.

As the screen filled with a sitcom he didn't recognize, he popped the top on the beer and took a deep swallow. Generally, Lucas wasn't a television kind of guy, but tonight he needed something to keep his mind off a pregnant blonde with warm blue eyes.

He focused on the sitcom and by nine had finished his beer and decided to call it a night. The next morning brought more of the same. The news didn't broadcast a missing pregnant woman report, and the moment Jane opened Loretta's door to his knock, he knew that she still didn't remember anything.

"Sleep well?" he asked.

"Actually, I slept like a baby," she replied.

She didn't look like a baby. The T-shirt she wore that pronounced Baby on Board pulled across the fullness of her breasts, and the maternity jeans they'd bought fit snug on her long, lean legs.

He could smell her, the clean scent of citrus shampoo and a fragrant soap. Every muscle in his body tensed. "You ready to leave?" he asked, his tone sharper than he'd intended.

"Just let me get a coat." She disappeared down the hallway.

She returned wearing the coat he'd loaned her the day before and together they left the apartment building. A cold wind blew from the north as they hurried to his car in the lot.

"What's the plan?" she asked once they were in the car and he'd started the engine.

"First we're going to take a ride around the area where I found you to see if that jiggles your memory," he said. "Then we'll head over to the office and see what Micah and Troy have found out about that symbol."

"I've disrupted your life. You must be sick of me already."

He turned to look at her, realizing that his sharp tone with her earlier hadn't gone unnoticed. "Don't worry about it. I didn't have much of a life for you to disrupt."

He backed out of the parking space, surprised that his own words swept that whisper of loneliness through him once again. What was the matter with him? He clenched the steering wheel more tightly, irritated by the wayward direction of his thoughts.

"Where exactly are we?" she asked as he pulled out on the street. "I mean, I know we're in Kansas City, but nothing looks familiar."

"Downtown is south of us. We're at the northern edges of the city," he replied. "The area where I found you is called Oak Grove Estates, upper-middle-class homes and a nice neighborhood. Ring a bell?"

"No." She frowned and stared out the window. "But I remember running and running before I got into that car to rest."

"Maybe we'll go by a house or a landmark that you recognize," he said. He wasn't sure what else to do. Somehow they needed to stimulate her mind to remember what had happened to her, and it wasn't happening in the safety of Loretta's apartment.

"Maybe," she agreed, and fell silent.

It didn't take long for them to reach Oak Grove. Lucas drove slowly down the street where two nights before he'd repossessed the car and held his breath for an "aha" moment from her.

But it didn't come. She stared out the window with desperation shining from her eyes. Thinking about the fact that she'd said she remembered running, he worked outward from the house where he'd found her, driving down street after street in the general area.

"It's no good," she finally said. "Nothing looks

familiar." Her voice held a wealth of disappointment. She released a weary sigh. "I'm beginning to think I'll never remember who I am or what happened."

"You can't give up," he replied. "It's just going to take some time, Jane. We have to be patient."

"I have to be patient, but you don't have to be," she replied. She looked at him. "Maybe it would be best if you did just drop me off at a motel, front me some money and let me figure this out on my own. You don't owe me anything. I'm not your problem. I'm just a stranger you happened to stumble on by accident."

It would be easy to do as she suggested, just pull into the parking lot of the nearest motel, pay for a week or two of lodging and drop her off and forget her. But he knew he wouldn't forget anything. She'd haunt him forever. He'd worry about what had happened to her, to her baby. He'd wonder where she was and how she fared. Nope, that simply wasn't an option right now.

He shot her a quick glance and then returned his gaze back to the road. "Don't be silly. I'm not about to drop you off someplace and just drive away and let you figure this out on your own." He thought he heard a little sigh of relief from her.

"Don't worry about me, Jane," he continued. "Sooner or later we'll find out who you are and what's happened to you. Until that happens, I'm here for you. I have no intention of walking away."

He glanced at her again, just in time to see her offer him one of those amazing smiles of hers. As he focused back on his driving, he had a feeling he was already in too deep where Jane was concerned.

THE RECOVERY INC. OFFICE was nicely decorated with two large desks and a waiting area with a leather sofa and matching chair. As Jane and Lucas entered, she beelined for the sofa and sank down to ease her aching back.

It seemed as if her baby's favorite position was sitting on her spine. Her lower back hurt most of the time.

"Troy and Micah should be here any minute," Lucas said as he walked over to the phone and punched the button to check the messages.

There was only one—a man calling about a missing cigar boat that he suspected had been stolen by his ex-son-in-law. He left a phone number with an area code Jane didn't recognize.

She felt ridiculously nervous about meeting his partners. It was as if she were Lucas's girlfriend and desperately wanted to make a good impression on his family. Of course, that was ridiculous. She was nothing more than a burden to him and it didn't matter whether his partners liked her or not.

"You want something to drink?" he asked.

"No, I'm fine," she replied.

At that moment the front door opened and a tall, good-looking man entered. Lucas introduced Jane to Micah Stone. He smiled and shook her hand warmly, then gestured her back down on the sofa.

"Lucas has told me a little about what's going on," he said as he shrugged out of his coat and hung it on the coat tree next to theirs. "I did some research on that symbol and have some things for you both to look at." He pulled several folded sheets of paper from his pocket.

As he sat on one side of her, Lucas sat on the other. She was flanked on either side by enough lean muscle and testosterone to feel as if the world could come to an end and somehow she'd survive.

"The all-seeing eye has quite a place in history," he said. "Generally it is a symbol of the protective power of a Supreme Being," Micah said. "In Mexican culture it's been used as a talisman against evil. Its origin can be traced back to Egyptian mythology and the Eye of Horus."

He opened up one of the sheets of paper and handed it to Lucas. "Did it look like this?"

Jane caught a glimpse of the picture and quickly closed her eyes. She didn't want to see it again, didn't understand what that symbol had to do with her and why it evoked such fear in her heart.

"Not exactly," Lucas replied. "It wasn't a pyramid. It wasn't like what's on the dollar bill, it was just a triangle." Micah handed him another sheet of paper. "That's it," he said.

Jane looked at Micah. "What is it?"

"It took me a while to find anything locally, but I finally found a church that uses the symbol kind of like their logo."

"A church?" Jane frowned. What on earth could a church have to do with her current situation?

"The Church of Enlightenment, to be exact," Micah said.

"And what did you find out about this church?" Lucas asked.

"Big church with a healthy, multidenominational congregation. The church owns about a hundred acres of land north of here. It's open to the public, but they have a small compound there that's a gated community of sorts."

"A gated community. That sounds rather odd," Lucas said with a frown.

"The church itself seems a bit odd," Micah said. "I didn't have time to do a lot of research. But from what information I was able to gather, the church is headed by a man known only as The Prophet, who gives the sermon each Sunday and remains a sort of mysterious father figure."

"Can you say cult?" Lucas said drily.

"I don't know about that," Micah replied. "I'd have to have a lot more information than what I have to make that kind of call."

"Just because we saw that symbol on the back of the van door doesn't mean the people who tried to grab me at the store are in any way related to this church," Jane said.

"That's true," Lucas said, his frustration obvious in his voice. "But you react strongly to that seeing eye and there's got to be a reason for it."

"Maybe I was as scared as a baby by a big hairy eyeball," she offered with a touch of humor.

Lucas laughed and shook his head. "I'm glad somebody still has a sense of humor about all this."

"You didn't notice anything else about the van?" Micah asked.

Lucas shook his head with a grim expression. "It was just a plain white panel van. Everything happened so fast." His frown deepened, as if irritated with himself for not doing more, for not seeing more.

At that moment the front door whooshed open and the third partner of the business walked in. Lucas introduced her to Troy Sinclair and for the next few minutes the three men talked about Recovery Inc. business.

As they talked she found herself watching them with interest. Loretta had told her that the three men had been best buddies when they'd all been Navy SEALs and that their close relationship had continued into civilian life.

Their friendship showed in the easy way they spoke to each other, in the way they could almost finish each other's thoughts. There was respect there, as well as the warmth of men who cared about each other.

Did she have a friend someplace? A girlfriend who she'd met for lunch or gone shopping with? A woman who had known her secrets and who had shared her laughter and her tears?

Where was that friend now? Was she worried about Jane? It was going on forty-eight hours that

Jane had been missing from her life. Didn't anyone care? A wave of despair rushed through her.

It was only when she heard her name that she focused on the three men once again. "I checked with Wendall. There have been no missing persons reports in the last twenty-four hours that match Jane," Lucas told his partners. "I plan on checking in with him again tomorrow morning."

"He didn't ask why you wanted to know?" Micah asked with a lift of one dark eyebrow.

"He asked. I didn't tell him," Lucas replied. "Jane has a feeling that in going to any authorities she could be putting herself in more danger than she's already in."

All three men turned to look at her and she felt the heat of a blush in her cheeks. "I can't explain it," she said. "I know it sounds irrational, but the idea of going to the police terrifies me."

"With what happened yesterday at the store, I'm willing to give it some time before going to the police, but I've told Jane if she doesn't recover her memories soon, eventually we might not have any other choice than to go to the authorities," Lucas said.

Even though Jane knew he was right, a shiver of dread worked through her at the thought. Why was she afraid of the police? Was she some kind of criminal? She couldn't imagine that being the case.

As she'd told Lucas when they'd first met, she might not know who she was, but she knew *what* she was. She'd bet her life she'd never been in trouble with the law in her life.

It was almost noon when they finally left the Recovery Inc. offices. The November air had chilled while they'd been inside and there was a faint scent of impending snow.

Thanksgiving was two weeks away. Would she be home by then? Would she be having turkey and stuffing surrounded by friends and loved ones, or would she still be struggling to figure out who she was and where she belonged?

Minutes later she and Lucas were back in his car and headed to Loretta's. "I'll drop you off at the apartment. Then I'll be back around dinnertime," Lucas said.

She didn't ask where he might be going or what he was going to do. She knew there was nothing more they could do to get her memory back. At the moment it seemed as if all she needed was some time. But how much time would it take before Lucas was sick of her and her problems?

It was a silent drive back to Loretta's. "You've gotten quiet," Lucas said as he turned the key in Loretta's door.

"I was just thinking about Thanksgiving and won-dering if I'd be home by then." She leaned against the wall in the hallway. "Do you and Loretta have a big feast that day?"

"Actually, we do. It's the one holiday that Loretta never works. She does the turkey and stuffing and makes sweet potatoes and pies and we invite some friends over."

He took a step closer to her and raised a hand and touched her cheek. "I'll do everything in my power to make sure that you're home for Thanksgiving," he said softly.

His warm fingers lingered on her cheek and Jane's breath caught in her chest. There was a look in his eyes that made her think he was going to kiss her and she was stunned by how much she wanted him to.

She raised a hand to capture his, not wanting him to draw away from her, but rather wanting him to fall into her, to wrap her in his arms and pull her as close as he possibly could.

She closed her eyes as he came closer, his mouth mere inches from hers. She leaned forward, wanting…needing the contact with him. And then his mouth touched hers.

Hot and tender, his soft lips plied hers in a kiss that didn't just warm her mouth, but sizzled a wave of warmth through her entire body.

It wasn't until he pulled her closer and her tummy bumped into him that he jerked back from her. "Sorry. That was inexcusable." He drew a deep breath as if to steady himself.

She took hold of his arm. "I can excuse it," she said. "In fact, if you wanted to do it again, I wouldn't have any problems excusing you." She couldn't believe her forwardness, but it wasn't just gratitude she felt for him, it was a white-hot attraction that had her half-giddy.

She was afraid she might have offended him, but he gave her a sexy half grin that only increased his appeal. "That was very nice, but we can't lose sight of the fact that there's probably a man in your life." His gaze shot pointedly down to her stomach.

"I don't think so," she said. "I can't explain it, Lucas, but I think I was alone before all this began."

He sighed and tucked a strand of her hair behind her ear, then opened the door to Loretta's apartment. "Get some rest," he said. "I'll see you later this evening."

He turned and nearly ran down the hall away from her. How foolish was she? A pregnant woman with no memory making passes at a hot guy who'd already said he had no interest in getting married or becoming a father.

How foolish was she to think that he'd even want to kiss her again. With a new depression settling over her shoulders she turned and went into the apartment.

Chapter Six

The kiss had been a major mistake. The taste of her sweet, lush lips haunted Lucas for the remainder of the day.

He'd left Loretta's apartment, gone straight back to his car and headed out to the Church of Enlightenment compound. He had no idea if it had been somebody from the church who had tried to grab Jane at the store, but the fact that the church used the seeing-eye symbol as a kind of trademark was the only lead they had.

The Church of Enlightenment was located at the very northern edges of Kansas City, about ten miles from the neighborhood where Lucas had found Jane in the car.

It seemed unlikely that Jane would have been able to walk ten miles in her condition that night, but he wasn't willing to rule out the possibility altogether. There were stories in the news all the time about people accomplishing all kinds of impossible feats when in danger.

The church itself was a huge building with amazing stained-glass windows and a sign across the door that welcomed all who came for spiritual nourishment.

He didn't bother going inside; in fact, didn't even leave his car. What interested him more than the church itself were the buildings in a gated area behind it.

There was a massive three-story home, several other low, flat buildings, a construction site with a foundation poured and fields as far as the eye could see. All of it was surrounded by tall, sturdy fencing designed to keep people out.

There was no question that religion could be big business, but this particular church didn't seem to be affiliated with any others or have an organized base. He made a mental note to ask Micah to see if he could find a list of the board of directors or whatever governed the money obviously flowing into this church.

He pulled up to the gate, but there was no guard on duty and the heavy iron fencing was locked.

Surely this couldn't have anything to do with Jane, he thought. Even if he were able to get a list of names of all the people in the congregation, there was no way he could pinpoint who had been responsible for the attack at the store.

It just didn't make sense. Maybe the sign he'd seen in the back of that van had nothing to do with this church. He just couldn't make the pieces fit.

He left the church and went back to the Recovery

Inc. office where Troy was inside working on the financial records for the company.

The two men talked about Jane and both agreed that time was what she needed most of all. Eventually something would trigger her memories, and in the meantime there wasn't much any of them could do.

While Lucas would love to know who had tried to grab her and why, the odds of figuring it out were not in his favor.

It was nearly four when Lucas left the office. But instead of heading home, he drove to the Sandbox, a bar and grill he frequented on a regular basis.

It was dark and smoky and the perfect place for a man to sit and drink a beer without being bothered by anyone. Even though Lucas had been coming here for years, he knew nothing about the bartender except that his name was Joe and he poured a perfect Scotch and soda.

Joe nodded to him as he took a stool at the bar and in the blink of an eye Lucas had his drink in front of him. He curled his fingers around the cold glass as he thought once again of kissing Jane.

He didn't know her real name, but he liked her sense of humor. He liked the fact that despite everything that had happened to her she hadn't melted down into a hysterical mess.

She represented everything he didn't want in his life, a woman who would want a husband, a woman beginning a family. Kissing her had been a major mistake. Even if she were single and as alone as she thought she might be, he had absolutely nothing to offer her.

Her mouth had been tempting before he'd tasted it, but with that single taste, his desire had winged out of control. He'd wanted to back her up against the wall and explore her mouth further. He'd wanted to cup her full breasts in his hands and feel their warmth, then take her hips and press them against his.

He clenched the cold drink glass tighter. She was vulnerable at the moment, and he'd be all kinds of a bastard to take advantage of that vulnerability.

Still, the thought of kissing her again filled him with an anticipation he hadn't felt for a very long time, and that bothered him. She bothered him in a way no woman ever had.

He finished his drink, then nursed a second one until just after seven, reluctant to share the evening meal with Loretta and Jane. Instead he filled up on nuts and pretzels, and wound up making small talk with a salesman from New Jersey who was in town for a convention.

Darkness had fallen when he finally left the Sandbox and headed back to his apartment. After sitting in the smoky confines of the bar, he wanted to shower before checking in with Jane and Loretta.

The minute he opened his apartment door he sensed something amiss. He froze in the doorway and looked around the living room, every muscle in his body on alert.

Lucas was an orderly man. Troy and Micah often teased him about having more than his share of obsessive-compulsive disorder when it came to his living space.

He pulled his gun as he saw that the magazines in the middle of the coffee table had been moved a fraction of an inch to the right and the papers at his desk weren't quite in the same position they'd been in before he'd left.

Even the picture of him and Loretta wasn't in the exact same place that it had been before he'd left that morning. Close, but no cigar.

Somebody had been in here. He gripped the gun more tightly and moved stealthily across the living-room floor. A glance into the kitchen showed nobody there. Then he headed down the hallway toward his bedroom.

His closet door was open just an inch. He knew he'd closed it completely after he'd gotten his clothes out that morning. He had an obsession about open doors and cabinets, and always made sure they were closed after he used them.

Somebody had been in here and it was obvious they hadn't wanted him to know about their presence. They'd been good. Somebody less observant would never have known anyone had been inside the place. But he knew, and the thought sent a cold chill through him.

It took him only minutes to know that there was nobody inside the place now. But somebody had been there. The words went around and around in his head.

He stood in the center of the living room, his thoughts racing to make sense of it. Why would any-one want to snoop around his apartment? Nothing appeared to be missing so it hadn't been a burglary.

Jane.

Her name thundered in his head. Had this been about Jane? Perhaps it was somebody looking for her or evidence of where she might be?

He hadn't gotten a license plate number from the van the day before at the store, but had somebody gotten his? And had that somebody used that infor-mation to find out who he was and where he lived in hopes that Jane would be here?

Time to move, he thought. He stared at the photo of himself and his sister. It wouldn't take a lot of digging for them to learn about Loretta.

A question here or there to one of the people in the apartment complex and they would know that Lucas and Loretta were siblings. It wouldn't take a rocket scientist to suspect that Lucas might have stashed Jane with his sister.

What was going on? Who was Jane and why did these people want her? What in the hell was going on?

He returned to the bedroom, where he packed a duffel bag, then left the apartment. A glance around the hallway showed nobody around and he hurried to Loretta's and let himself in using his key.

He dropped his duffel just inside the front door

and headed for the kitchen where he could hear the sound of Jane and Loretta's laughter.

The two women were seated at the table. The dinner dishes had been cleaned up, but they each had a piece of cake in front of them. Jane had a glass of milk and Loretta had coffee. Both of them looked relaxed and happy.

"Lucas!" Jane said as he walked into the room. Her eyes shone with a bright warmth that stirred something inside him. "I was wondering if you were going to show up this evening."

"Have you eaten?" Loretta asked.

He nodded. "Loretta, were you in my place today?"

"No, why?" She looked at him curiously.

"Jane, you need to pack a bag. I've got to move you out of here."

The warmth in her eyes fled and was replaced with fear. "Why? What do you mean?"

"What's happened?" Loretta asked as she stood from the table.

"Somebody was in my apartment today. I think they were snooping around to find Jane." Jane's eyes widened at his words.

"But surely nobody knows she's here," Loretta said.

"Maybe not yet, but eventually they'll figure it out. They probably saw the picture I have of the two of us together. If they figure out who you are, eventually they'll check to see if she's here."

Jane got up from the table. "I'll go get my things." Her voice was slightly shaky.

"Wait, Jane." Loretta placed an arm around Jane's shoulders. "I'll get you an overnight bag." Together the two women left the kitchen.

Lucas returned to the living room to wait for Jane, his mind still filled with possibilities and suppositions.

Right now the only thing he could do was act defensively, try to minimize risk without knowing exactly from what direction the danger might come.

He picked up his own bag as Jane and Loretta returned to the living room. Jane had on her coat and clutched a small black bag. "Where are you taking me?" she asked. There was a wealth of dread in her voice.

"A safe place," he replied.

"The safe house?" Loretta asked and he nodded.

Jane looked at him curiously. "I'll explain on the way," he told her, then looked at his sister. "I'll call you."

"Am I in danger?" Loretta asked.

Lucas frowned. "I don't think so. It's apparent whoever was in my apartment wasn't looking for a confrontation of any kind. They got in and out while I was away."

Jane grabbed Loretta's hand. "I hope I haven't brought danger to your doorstep. I'm so sorry about all of this."

"Don't worry," Loretta assured her. "Hasn't Lucas told you I'm tough?"

"Just make sure there's no sign that she was ever here in the apartment," Lucas said as he opened the door and peered down the hallway. Seeing nobody around, he motioned Jane out the door.

Neither of them said a word as they headed for the door that would lead outside into the cold, dark, early-November night.

When they reached the door, Lucas told her to wait, then stepped out and looked around. Unfortunately the darkness made it difficult for him to see if anyone was hiding in the shadows, cloaked by the night.

He drew his gun, unwilling to be surprised without the protection of his weapon. He stepped back inside the door and grabbed Jane's arm. "Stay right next to me. We're going directly to my car."

He felt the tremble of her body as he pulled her close against his side. He felt bad that she was scared, but better scared and on guard than oblivious and vulnerable.

He didn't breathe again until they were both safely in his car. As he started the engine once again he scanned the area, looking for any threat that might come out of the darkness.

Nothing. He saw nobody lurking about, nobody sitting in a nearby vehicle. But that didn't mean they weren't there.

Pulling out of the parking lot, he kept his gaze focused on the rearview mirror, looking for any other car that might follow.

Even though he saw none, he didn't feel safe, wouldn't feel safe until they reached the house and he was certain that nobody had followed them there.

A tense silence filled the car as he drove, constantly watching the rear- and side-view mirrors. He was grateful for her silence as he needed all his concentration on the road.

He drove down neighborhood streets, turning first left, then right at random in an effort to identify whether they had a tail or not.

For thirty minutes he drove first one direction, then another and finally felt comfortable that nobody was following them. His tense muscles began to relax and the adrenaline that had pumped through him from the moment he'd walked in his front door ebbed slightly.

"The safe house is a ranch house out in the country," he finally said, breaking the silence that had filled the car. "It's owned by a dummy corporation that can't be traced back to Recovery Inc. The only people who know where it is are my partners and their girlfriends, Loretta and Wendall Kincaid, the chief of police. You'll be safe there until we can figure all this out."

"The only way we're going to get anywhere is if I get my memories back, and that doesn't seem to be happening," she said, her frustration obvious. "I'm sorry, Lucas. I'm so sorry about all of this."

"There's no need for you to apologize," he assured her. "This won't be the first time Recovery Inc. has helped somebody in trouble."

He frowned and tightened his hands around the steering wheel. Twice in recent months the safe house had been used, first by Micah, who had hidden out there with Caylee while they fought false murder charges brought against them both. Then the ranch house had been used by Troy to keep his girlfriend, Brianna, safe when a stalker had been after her.

Both men had found love while in the safe house, but there was no way Lucas would fall victim to the same thing. He glanced over at Jane, who had her fingers splayed across her belly, as if to protect the life within.

She belonged somewhere, to somebody. And even if she didn't, he told himself he wasn't interested in any kind of a relationship with her and the baby she carried.

It didn't matter that he'd liked kissing her, that he definitely wouldn't mind kissing her again…and more. Even though he didn't know her real name, he had a feeling that Jane was a forever kind of woman, that she'd want the picket fence and a husband by her side. She'd want family barbecues and a brother or sister for the baby she carried.

She definitely didn't strike him as the type who would be ready for an affair with no strings attached and no promises of forever. He reached up and rubbed the back of his neck, where he could feel the ridge of an old scar.

An ancient wave of anger welled up inside him as he dropped his hand back to the steering wheel. A vision of his father entered his mind.

Lucas couldn't remember a time when Roger Washington's face wasn't twisted and red with rage.

He couldn't remember a kind touch, a loving glance. All of Lucas's memories of his father were filled with pain, both physical and mental.

That was his legacy. And that was what Lucas would never take a chance of passing on. He couldn't be a bad husband if he never married. And he couldn't be a brutal father if he never had children.

The safe house had brought love to his two partners, but there was no way in hell Lucas would allow himself to fall victim to the same emotion.

JANE STARED OUT THE WINDOW at the dark landscape. They'd left the city behind and were traveling on roads with no streetlights. The houses were discernible only by the faint spill of light from windows, and they were getting farther and farther apart.

Two days ago, if Lucas had driven her out here in the middle of nowhere she would have been terrified. But in the two days she'd spent with him she'd come to trust him implicitly.

The idea that she'd brought danger to the young woman who had opened her home and her heart to her broke Jane's heart. She'd die if anything happened to Loretta because of her.

Who were these people? And why, oh, why couldn't she remember anything? She desperately needed her memory. She needed her identity to make sense of everything that had happened.

She sat up straighter in her seat as he turned down a narrow gravel road. Eventually they came to a clearing where she could see the dark outline of a house with tall trees on either side.

Where would this all end? she thought with despair. What if the people who had tried to grab her at the store somehow found her here? Then where would she go?

"Stop worrying," he said as if he could read her thoughts.

She cast him a nervous smile. "I can't help it."

He pulled up in front of the house, killed the engine and turned to look at her, his eyes dark and glittering in the faint illumination from the dashboard. "You'll be safe here. And who knows, maybe in the next couple of days your memories will come back."

"I hope so," she said fervently. She changed positions in the seat, her back aching with a dull throb. "That night when you found me in the car and I realized I had some sort of amnesia, I was sure that once I got a good night's sleep I'd wake up and everything would be all right. But I've had two good nights of sleep now and still nothing."

"It's only been a couple of days," he said. He pulled the keys from the ignition and turned off the lights. "Come on, let's get settled inside."

As they got out of the car, the unusually cold wind seemed to blow right through her, chilling her to the bones. But she knew it wasn't the wind that made her cold; rather it was fear of the unknown.

She felt somewhat better when they were in the house and Lucas had turned on the lights. The living room was pleasant, although decorated as impersonally as a motel room.

"The kitchen is in here," he said. "I'll head out first thing in the morning and get some groceries." The kitchen was large and airy and decorated with bright yellow accents.

From the kitchen he led her down a hallway. "You can stay in here," he said as he stopped at the first doorway. "The bathroom is across the hall. I'll stay in the bedroom in the back." He set her overnight bag on the double bed. "Don't look so scared. You're going to be just fine."

The warmth of his deep voice helped ease some of the tension that had tightened her muscles since the moment he'd walked into Loretta's kitchen and told her to pack a bag. She shrugged off her coat and tossed it on the chair just inside the bedroom door.

"I just wish I knew what was going on," she said softly. She sat on the edge of the bed and rubbed her lower back with one hand.

"One thing you don't have to worry about is support from me," he said. "If I wasn't in until the end before, I am now." His eyes narrowed. "They made a big mistake when they came into my apartment and invaded my privacy." He frowned. "Are you all right?"

She nodded. "Just a little backache. It's no big deal."

"It's not labor pains, is it?"

She nearly laughed out loud at the horrified look on his face. The tough ex–navy SEAL with a gun on his shoulder looked scared to death at the idea of a baby's birth.

"No, it isn't labor," she assured him. "Just a backache. It will probably be gone by morning."

"Then I'll just say good-night," he said. "If you need anything I'm just down the hall." He disappeared from the doorway.

She wanted to call him back. She wanted him to stay with her throughout the long, lonely night, hold her in his arms to keep away any nightmares that might try to rear their ugly heads.

Instead she got up from the bed and closed the door, then pulled her nightgown from the bag. It was after nine and she was tired. She took her nightgown and toothbrush into the bathroom across the hall and changed, then brushed her teeth and stared at her reflection in the mirror. "Who are you?" she asked the woman who stared back at her.

With a tired sigh she turned away from the mirror. Even though she was exhausted, she feared the night to come.

Even more fearful was the idea that she'd sleep soundly and wake up the next morning with nothing changed, no memories returning.

Lucas had told her he was in until the end, but she knew if too much time went by he would start encouraging her to go to the police. And although she didn't understand it, that idea horrified her.

Did she have a husband who was a cop? An abusive man she'd run to escape? Or was she wanted by the law and running from a prison sentence? There were so many questions without an answer in sight.

As she left the bathroom she heard the faint sound of Lucas's voice coming from the back bedroom and assumed he was on the phone with somebody. Perhaps telling his partners of this latest development, she thought.

She turned off the light and got into the unfamiliar bed. Lying on her back, she watched the shadows of tree limbs dancing in the moonlight on the ceiling and tried to empty her mind of the million questions that played there.

She must have fallen asleep because the next time she opened her eyes, the sun was shining through the window and the scent of frying bacon and fresh coffee hung in the air.

She kept her eyes closed, for a moment fantasizing that it was her husband in the kitchen preparing a morning meal for his beloved pregnant wife. And after breakfast, he'd rub her aching back with loving hands as he whispered how much he loved her.

Squeezing her eyes more tightly closed, she tried to summon an image of the man, but all that came to her mind was a vision of Lucas.

Her mouth burned as she remembered the taste of his lips, the fire they had ignited in her, a flame of desire. She'd only known him for a couple of days and yet she was more than a little bit crazy about him.

Was it possible she didn't want to go to the authorities because she knew that would be the end of their time together?

It was a shameful thought and it pulled her out of bed and across the hall for a shower—a cold shower to cool thoughts of Lucas and his sinfully soft lips.

Once she was dressed, she felt better prepared to face whatever the day might bring and the man who was precariously close to owning her heart.

"Ah, I thought I heard you up and about." Lucas greeted her as she walked into the kitchen. She stopped short and for a moment forgot how to breathe.

He stood at the stove, clad only in a pair of jogging pants that rode low on his lean hips. His black hair was boyishly tousled, but there was nothing boyish about his broad muscled chest or the stubble of dark whiskers across his jaw. He looked hot and she felt his heat warming every part of her body.

"You hungry?" he asked.

"You have no idea," she muttered more to herself than to him.

"I have to admit I'm not the best of cooks, but I figured I could rustle up some bacon and eggs. Sit and I'll get you a glass of juice," he instructed.

She slid into a chair at the table and tried to look at anything but him. "You must have gotten up and out early."

"There's a twenty-four-hour grocery store not far from here. I got up at dawn and got enough supplies in for a couple of days. How do you like your eggs? I'd recommend scrambled."

She smiled. "Scrambled is fine."

He turned toward the refrigerator and she saw the scars on his back. They were faint, but discernible, and crisscrossed the expanse of his back. "Lucas, what happened to you?" He whirled around to face her. "Your back. What happened to your back?" she asked.

A myriad of emotions played across his features before they finally settled on calm acceptance. He turned back to grab a carton of eggs from the fridge. "My father happened to me," he replied after a long hesitation.

She stared at him for a long moment as his words sank in. "He beat you?" Her heart ached for him as she realized that must have been what he'd meant when he'd told her it had always been him and Loretta against the world.

"Just about every day of my life until I turned eighteen and joined the navy." He cracked several eggs into a bowl and offered her a tight smile. "He was a miserable bastard who for whatever reason decided early in my life that I was the source of his misery."

"Did he drink? Was he drunk when he beat you?" She couldn't imagine a parent doing that to a child unless he was out of his mind on drugs or alcohol. And even then it was unimaginable.

"No. He was always stone-cold sober whenever he beat me."

"What about Loretta? Did he beat her, too?"

"Never touched her." He poured the egg mixture into an awaiting skillet. "Maybe he instinctively knew that if he did, I'd kill him." He said the words matter-of-factly and Jane wondered what kind of scars had been left behind that couldn't be seen with the naked eye.

"Loretta was only about five years old the first time she crept into my room after I'd gotten a beating." He pushed the button on the toaster. "She had a wet washcloth and placed it over my forehead, then held my hand until I finally went to sleep." He smiled again, this smile with more warmth. "Even then she was taking care of the sick and wounded. After each and every beating I got, it was Loretta who came into my room to bring me water or rub salve on my back."

"What about your mother? Where was she when all this was happening?" Jane asked.

"She was sitting in her chair, or making dinner or watching television. She was emotionally disengaged. She neither encouraged him nor stopped him."

"Did your father beat her?" she asked.

"Not that I remember. She didn't seem particularly afraid of him. She just didn't seem to love Loretta and me enough to fight for us. For a long time after I was grown I wasn't sure who I hated more, him or her." He picked up a spoon and stirred the eggs and smiled at her once again. "Don't look so stricken, Jane. I survived and I'm probably stronger for it."

The toast popped up, and as he buttered it, Jane's heart opened wider to him. There were other ways to gain strength than to survive a horrendous childhood, she thought.

"I can't imagine being hit by my parents," she finally said. "My mother always said she could tell when I was fibbing because I'd tug on the end of my hair, but I was always punished with a time-out or grounding, never hit."

She looked at him in surprise. "I remembered that." She frowned and concentrated on the faint memory that stirred inside her head. "My mother's name was Bernice, but everyone called her Bernie."

"And what was her last name?" He stared at her intently.

She reached for it, trying desperately to put a last name to the woman's face that filled her mind, but it was no good. The vision fell away and no matter how hard she tried she couldn't summon it again. She shook her head. "No, it's gone." She sighed in frustration.

"It's okay," he assured her as he ladled the food on plates. "It's a good sign that you had even a single memory. Maybe that means they'll all start coming back." He placed her plate in front of her. "And it's good information to know, about the hair-tugging," he teased.

She laughed and picked up her fork. "I can't imagine ever lying to you. You're the only one I trust completely right now."

"I'm the only one you know right now," he returned as he joined her at the table.

"True, but I have a feeling if there were a dozen people in my life, you'd still be the one I trusted most. In fact, I'm thinking when my little boy is born, I'll name him Luke, after you."

Any teasing light that had warmed his eyes vanished. "Don't, Jane."

"Don't what?" she asked.

"Don't make me into some kind of a hero." His eyes grew hard and a knot pulsed in his jaw. "I'm just the man who is stuck with you until we can figure out where you really belong."

She stared at him for a long moment. She might have lost all her memories, but she still remembered what it felt like to be hurt.

Chapter Seven

"I'm heading in to the office to meet with Troy and Micah," Lucas said three days later as Jane sat at the kitchen table, drinking a glass of orange juice. "I should be back by dinnertime."

He needed to check in with his partners and stop by his sister's place, but more than anything he needed to escape from Jane and the tension that had built to intolerable proportions in the last three days of isolation.

She nodded. "I'll have something ready for dinner."

It had quickly become habit that she cooked dinner and they both did the cleanup afterward. The domestic nature of their time in the house was definitely starting to get under his skin.

"Thanks," he replied. "Lock up behind me. I'll see you later." He grabbed his coat and pulled it on, then walked out the front door and into the unusually cold, gray day.

There was a taste of snow in the air. The weathermen on the news the night before had talked about the possibility of an early snowstorm. Just what he needed—to be snowed in with the woman who was slowly driving him out of his mind.

He started the car and as he waited for the engine to warm up, he stared at the house and thought of the woman inside.

She'd been unusually quiet, and he knew she'd been hurt by his words at breakfast that first morning. But he'd needed to ground her in reality. She'd looked at him as if he were the man he wished to be instead of the man he feared he was, and that had scared him.

They'd spent the three days playing cards and Monopoly to pass the time. She was good at poker, but lacked the killer instinct to win at the board game. She'd teased him about closing cabinet doors and meticulously arranging things in an orderly fashion, and he hadn't taken offense. In truth, he found the teasing charming.

They were no closer to finding out who might be after her, but more memories had resurfaced. She'd remembered a high school dance and a trip to the Kansas City Zoo. She'd also remembered her father's funeral and then burying her mother two years later. They were bits and pieces of a life returning in brief glimpses that had yet to reveal the information they most needed—her name.

Still, he knew now that it was probably just a

matter of days before her memory completely returned and then she'd be out of his life for good.

What he didn't understand was why the idea of never seeing her again bothered him more than a little bit. Each evening as they'd sat in the living room watching television, his attention had been focused on her.

He loved the way she lifted her hair off her neck when she got too warm, how she unconsciously rubbed her tummy as if caressing the baby inside her.

The sound of her laughter filled him with a particular kind of joy he'd never felt before, and the worry that flirted darkly in her amazing eyes made him want to move heaven and earth to take it away.

He put the car into gear and pulled away from the house. Definitely time for some distance. How on earth had she managed to get so deep inside him in such a short space of time?

Unlike his sister, he'd never had a particularly soft spot for strays or the vulnerable, and yet something about Jane touched him in a way nobody ever had.

He tightened his hands around the steering wheel. He needed to get a grip. He glanced over to the small brown bag on the passenger seat. Inside was a drinking glass that Jane had used the night before.

He'd sneaked the glass into the bag and brought it out to the car last night after she'd gone to bed. He had a friend at the crime lab who could print it and run her through the AFIS. If she had a criminal record or had ever been fingerprinted for anything, the Automated Fingerprint Identification System would find her. He'd considered doing this before, but had dismissed the idea, hoping the situation would resolve itself.

He hadn't told her what he was going to do, knew that it would only add additional stress to an already-stressful situation. There was no question that he was intrigued by her adamant refusal to go to the police. At least by checking her fingerprints, within the next twenty-four to forty-eight hours he'd know if she had a record. And if she did, then they'd know her name.

Before dropping the glass off with his buddy, before checking in with his partners, he wanted to see Loretta. By the time he pulled into the apartment complex, the gray sky had begun to spit snow.

Today was Loretta's day off, and despite the fact that it was nearly ten o'clock when he knocked on her door, she greeted him still clad in her pajamas and with a coffee mug in hand.

She ushered him into the kitchen, where he poured himself a cup and sat at the table across from her.

"I heard the weatherman mention snow today and decided it was a good day to stay in my pajamas," she said. "How's it going? How is Jane?"

"Okay. She's started getting some memories back, although nothing about who she is or what happened to her. She's remembered fairly inconsequential things."

"But that's a good sign," Loretta exclaimed.

"That's what I told her. That's what I keep telling myself, that it's just a matter of time before she remembers everything."

"I kind of miss having her around." Loretta took a sip of her coffee and then continued. "She was good company. She has a great sense of humor. I like her."

"Yeah, well, it won't be long before she's back where she belongs."

"Maybe she shouldn't go back where she belongs," Loretta said. "I mean, she ran away for a reason."

Lucas frowned with a touch of irritation. He didn't want to think about that. He had to hang on to the idea that someplace out there Jane had a safe place to go and people who cared about her. "I'm just ready for this all to be over. I need to get back to my life."

Loretta crooked one of her dark eyebrows upward and smiled ruefully. "What life?"

"Ha, ha, very funny," Lucas replied drily.

"I'm not trying to be funny. You have my life and you have your partners' lives, but you don't have much of one of your own."

"It's a little early in the morning for a Dr. Phil moment," he replied. "Have you seen anyone suspicious lurking around the apartment building over the past couple of days?"

"No, and I wasn't finished talking about you,"

she replied. "Seriously, Lucas, at least it was nice to see you interacting with Jane. You like her. I know you do. I could tell by the way you looked at her. I know she probably has a life to get back to, but it's all made me think about how much I wish you'd find some nice woman to be a part of your life."

"I don't need anyone in my life," he replied. "Besides, you're one to talk. When was the last time you had a date?"

"Actually, I have one this Friday night." She smiled smugly.

Lucas leaned back in his chair and narrowed his eyes. "With who?"

"He's a really nice guy who works as a lab tech at the hospital. We've been spending our breaks together for the last month or so, and he finally asked me out."

"What's his name?" Lucas asked.

She shook her head. "Oh no, you don't. You are not going to check him out through whatever nefarious means you might have. I'll tell you his name on the day of the wedding."

Lucas stared at her in stunned surprise. "It's that serious?"

She laughed. "Not yet. But I am serious about you staying out of it." She leaned forward and covered one of his hands with her own. "I love you, Lucas, but you have to give me a little breathing room to find my own way when it comes to romance."

He knew she was right. "Just be careful. Make

sure you go someplace where there are other people." He bit his tongue before a full-blown lecture could escape. "And have a good time."

She smiled gratefully. "Thank you. I plan on it."

"I've got to get out of here," he said with a check of his watch. "I've got some errands to run before I get back to Jane." He stood, drained his coffee cup and carried it to the sink. "Call me Friday night when you get home, okay?"

"It might be late." She got up from the table to walk him to the door.

"That's all right. I'll sleep better knowing you're home safe and sound."

She walked with him to the front door. "You'll let me know what happens with Jane?"

"As soon as I know anything," he replied.

"Good. I'd like to keep in contact with her. She's a terrific woman, memory or no memory."

Minutes later as Lucas drove to the lab, he felt a new depression settle across his shoulders. His partners were both building new lives with women that they loved, and it was obvious Loretta was excited about her date on Friday night. Things were changing. Everyone seemed to be moving on with their lives while Lucas was being left behind.

He shoved the ridiculous thought from his mind as he pulled into the parking lot of a small café across from the Kansas City Crime Lab.

The lab itself was housed in a low, long brick building, but he'd arranged to meet his friend at the

Cornerstone Café, which was usually filled with people from the lab grabbing a bite to eat.

He spied Justin James seated at a booth in the back the minute he walked through the door. Loretta described Justin as the hottest science nerd on the face of the planet. Lucas didn't know about hot, but he knew the man ate, slept and breathed forensic science.

Justin raised a hand as he saw Lucas approach. With his other hand he picked up a cinnamon roll the size of New Jersey and took a bite.

"Sugar and science," Lucas said as he slid into the booth opposite the blond-haired man. "It's nice to see some things never change."

Justin shrugged. "As far as I'm concerned, change is vastly overrated. Now, to what do I owe the honor of this meeting?"

Lucas set the paper bag on the table. "This is a drinking glass. You should be able to lift a decent set of prints from it. I'd like you to run it through the AFIS and see if anything pops up."

"And what's in it for me?" Justin raised one of his blond eyebrows.

"Two dozen glazed from the bakery of your choice," Lucas replied.

"Done. It will take about twenty-four hours. I'll call you with any results."

"I appreciate it," Lucas said.

"Gonna tell me what this is all about?"

"Nope." Lucas signaled the waitress for a cup of

coffee. "And I'd prefer this to stay between you and me."

"I figured that without you saying," Justin said.

"How's work at the lab?"

"The one thing good about working in a crime lab is I never worry about job security. As long as there are bad people in the world, my job is relatively safe."

The two men visited briefly about work, sports and the weather; then Justin stood to get back to work and Lucas left, as well.

He checked in with Troy and Micah at the office, then decided to head back to the safe house and Jane. The snow was coming down in earnest and he turned on his wiper blades against the fat, wet flakes that obscured his vision and began to cover the street and grass.

He'd only gotten a block or so from the office building when he noticed a dark sedan two car lengths behind him. He turned down a residential street and watched his mirror. The sedan followed, and just behind it another black sports car.

Lucas turned again and watched as the sedan fell back and the sports car got behind him, tag-teaming him in an attempt to hide the fact that they were following him.

A surge of adrenaline filled him as he increased his speed and fishtailed around another corner to make sure that his assessment of the situation was correct. The two cars followed.

He stomped on the brakes and stared into the

rearview mirror at the front license of the car that nearly rear-ended him. JMV-237.

"JMV-237. JMV-237." He repeated it several times until he was sure he had it memorized; then he stepped on the gas and tightened his grip on the wheel as he set about losing the tails.

They were good. But he was better.

He rocked through the streets like a NASCAR driver, taking turns too fast for the road conditions and breaking the speed limits in his effort to evade them.

It took thirty minutes to finally ditch them. Still he drove aimlessly for another thirty minutes, constantly checking his mirror to make sure he'd lost them for good.

When he was confident that he wasn't being followed any longer, he headed to the house and Jane as he wondered again who the hell she was and why people were after her.

HER BACK HAD BOTHERED HER throughout the day. Jane was seated on the sofa with a pillow from the bedroom behind her for support when Lucas came inside.

Instantly she could tell that something had happened. She straightened. "I didn't hear you pull up out front," she said.

"I didn't. I pulled around to the back and parked in the garage." He sat on the chair across from her, energy rolling off him in waves. "I've got Troy and Micah dropping off a rental car later this evening."

"What happened?"

As he told her about being followed from the Recovery Inc. office, a new frustration coupled with a familiar fear edged through her.

"Who are these people and what do they want with me?" she cried in desperation.

"I don't know, but I'm hoping we'll have the name of one of them before the night is over. I got a license number of one of the cars that was following me and I put in a call to Wendall Kincaid."

"The chief of police?" she asked. As always, the idea of the police knowing anything about her made a nervous flutter in her stomach.

"Don't worry. I told him the driver of the car rear-ended me and I need his name to file an accident report." Lucas raked a hand through his hair and leaned back in the chair.

He looked exhausted, and a wave of guilt swept through Jane. "Maybe we should go to the police," she said, and heard the slight tremor in her voice. "This is getting so complicated and I'm sure you're sick to death of me."

He smiled, but she could tell it was slightly forced. "I'm not sick of you. I am sick of not knowing what's going on. I could maybe understand some crazy nut being after you…a stalker boyfriend or husband…but this isn't just a single individual. It's a whole group of people."

"Maybe I really am a spy," she said. "That's one of the things Loretta and I came up with. Of course we also thought I might be an undercover rock star or a high-class madame."

A whisper of a smile curved his lips and she saw him starting to relax. "I guess it's better to be a high class-madame than a low-class one."

She leaned back against the pillow once again. "I have discovered one important fact about myself today."

"What's that?"

"I don't like soap operas. When you feel like you're living one, the last thing you want to do is watch one."

"Your back still hurting?" he asked as she adjusted her position against the pillow.

She nodded. "It's just a dull ache. I think carrying around this baby weight is pulling on my spine. But it's fine. I'm fine. I made a pot of stew for dinner, but it's still simmering and won't be ready for another hour or so."

"That's all right. I'm not hungry. If you don't mind, I'm going back to the bedroom to make some phone calls. I'm expecting a fax soon and the machine is back there." He got up from the chair and she watched him disappear down the hallway.

As always when he left, he seemed to take some of the energy from the room, from her. She rubbed her stomach as she thought of the new events that had taken place.

The license plate number he'd managed to get was the first real clue they'd had that might yield answers, and she was surprised to realize she was conflicted about it.

On the one hand she wanted her life back, whatever that life might be. She hated the idea that she was taking advantage of Lucas and keeping him from his own life, but on the other hand she didn't want to tell him goodbye.

Was she reluctant to let go of him because she had nothing else to hang on to? Perhaps if she were completely truthful with herself she'd accept that that was part of it. But what was more difficult to accept was the fact that she didn't want to leave him because she was falling in love with him.

It was crazy. It was positively insane. She was carrying somebody's baby. She didn't even know her own name, but she knew what was in her heart and if felt like love.

She didn't believe that Lucas felt as if he was stuck with her, as he'd said at breakfast the first morning in the house. She wasn't sure what he felt about her. But if that kiss they'd shared and the odd moments when she felt his gaze lingering on her were any indication, he definitely felt something toward her that wasn't just a reluctant responsibility.

Twice she got up from the sofa and went into the kitchen to stir the stew, then stood at the window and watched the snow. It had finally tapered off to flurries, leaving behind less than an inch on the ground.

She'd returned to the living room and was back on the sofa some time later when Lucas came back into the living room and handed her a sheet of paper with a driver's license copied on it.

"Recognize him?" he asked as he sat next to her on the sofa.

She took the sheet of paper from him and stared at it. Charles Blankenship. He was fifty-eight years old, weighed two hundred pounds and was five feet eleven.

He had a severe, square jaw and brown eyes, his salt-and-pepper hair was cut military short and he wasn't smiling for the camera.

She frowned thoughtfully. "He looks vaguely familiar, but I don't know from where." She handed him back the sheet of paper. "Who is he?"

"One of the cars that followed me was registered to him. I think first thing in the morning I'm going to pay Mr. Charlie Blankenship a visit."

"I want to come with you."

"I'm not sure that's a good idea," he replied with a frown.

"It's the only idea we've got," she protested. "His picture looks familiar. Maybe seeing him in person will finally jiggle my memory. Besides, I'm not worried about my safety as long as I'm with you. It's my life, Lucas. Please let me be a part of things."

He stared at her for a long moment, and in the depths of his dark brown eyes she saw the same emotion that she'd seen moments before he'd kissed her. It was a yearning that made her breath catch in her throat and dried her mouth with sweet anticipation.

He leaned forward, as if drawn to her by an invisible thread, and she parted her lips, wanting him to kiss her again, needing to feel his warm, soft mouth against hers.

Abruptly he stood. "You think that stew is ready now?" His voice was deeper than usual.

She released her breath and nodded. The moment was broken, but it gave her a crazy new hope, the hope that somehow when this was all finished they might be together.

They had just finished eating when Troy and Micah arrived with the rental car. Jane made a pot of coffee as the three men sat at the table and Lucas caught them up on his chase that afternoon.

He showed them the faxed copy of Charles Blankenship's driver's license, but neither of them had any idea who the man was or why he'd be following Lucas.

"It has to be Jane," Lucas said. "They're looking for her."

She turned around from the sink as she felt the weight of three pairs of eyes on her. "I wish I could explain it. I wish I knew what was going on."

"Our plan is to talk to Charles Blankenship in the morning and ask him why he was following me," Lucas said as Jane joined them at the table.

Micah looked at her. "And you still don't want to go to the cops?"

She hesitated before replying. No, she didn't want to go to the police, but she also knew if that's what Lucas wanted her to do, then that's what she would do.

"Not yet," Lucas replied for her. She smiled at him gratefully. At least he wasn't so sick of her that he was willing to throw her to the dogs. Not yet.

"For whatever reason, Jane feels as if she'd be putting herself at risk by going to the cops and we're hoping before that becomes our only option her memory will return."

Micah nodded and tapped the picture of Charles Blankenship with the tip of a finger. "Want me to see what I can dig up on this guy before morning?"

"That would be great," Lucas replied. "You're better than anyone I know at digging up facts about people."

Micah grinned at the compliment, then looked at Troy. "We'd better get out of here so I can get to work."

The four of them rose from the table and walked to the front door. "Micah, Troy, thank you for all your help," Jane said. "I'm sure Lucas knows how lucky he is to have friends like you that he can depend on."

A niggling depression weighed her down as she told the men goodbye and went back to sit on the sofa as Lucas walked out with them.

She'd been missing almost six days and still nobody seemed to be looking for her. Why wasn't somebody worried about her? Why didn't anyone care that she was missing?

Was she so unimportant in this life that she could disappear for days...for a week...forever and nobody cared?

Chapter Eight

The house was quiet. Jane had gone to bed an hour earlier and Lucas sat at the kitchen table, worrying about everything he'd learned during the course of the evening.

Justin had called to tell him that there had been no hit on Jane's fingerprints, so that had been a bust.

And Lucas had almost kissed her again.

He frowned and stared out the window. He'd wanted to kiss her again so badly it had ached in his chest and burned in his blood.

Thank God he hadn't followed through on the impulse. Nothing good could come from him kissing her again.

Still, even now the scent of her remained in his head, the citrus-clean fragrance of her shampoo coupled with a faint, floral, feminine scent that drove him half-mad.

He hadn't just wanted to kiss her, he'd wanted to touch her skin, rub her belly and feel the kick of her son against his palm. The son she said she was going to name after him.

If he looked deep within himself, he had to recognize that he'd been touched by her words, and yet horrified at the same time. He didn't want a kid named after him and he definitely didn't want a woman looking at him with such trust, with something that looked like love.

His cell phone vibrated in his shirt pocket and he pulled it out, grateful for the disruption of his thoughts.

"Ready for a little bit of information?" Micah asked.

"Whatever you've got." Lucas leaned back in his chair.

"Charles Blankenship is an insurance salesman. No criminal record, nothing to indicate he's anything but a good, upstanding citizen. He's married and has two grown children, one grandchild. No financial issues, the usual credit card debt and a car loan, but nothing out of the ordinary."

Lucas bit back a sigh of frustration. "I was hoping for something different, something that might explain his interest in Jane."

"The only thing I discovered that I think you'll find interesting is that he's on the board of directors of the Church of Enlightenment."

A bolt of adrenaline flashed through Lucas, sitting him up straighter in his chair. "What?"

"The board consists of eight men and two

women. Charles is one of them. I don't know what it means, Lucas, but I'm going to do a little more digging into this church."

"Yeah, thanks. I'd appreciate it," Lucas replied thoughtfully. "I don't get it, Micah. Why would a church want Jane?"

"I don't know, buddy. We can't be sure it has anything to do with the church. The worst thing you can do is jump to conclusions without solid evidence. Right now, the fact that this Charles was chasing you and that Jane has an aversion to his church's logo could be nothing more than coincidence."

"And you really believe that?" Lucas asked drily.

"Not for one minute," Micah replied. Lucas could hear the grin in his buddy's voice.

Long after the two men hung up, Lucas remained at the table, trying to fit together pieces of the puzzle of Jane.

Was it just a coincidence that the logo the church used inspired an irrational fear in Jane and that the man who had been tailing Lucas was a member of the board of that church?

Why would a church be after Jane? It was the question that kept niggling at his brain. None of it made sense. Maybe Charles would be forthcoming in the morning when Lucas had a little visit with him. Yeah, right, and maybe tomorrow it would be warm enough to swim.

He got up from the table and checked the back

door to make sure it was securely locked, then turned out the lights and walked through the dark living room.

He checked the front door and headed down the hallway, but he'd only taken a couple of steps when he heard the sound of crying coming from Jane's room.

Just walk on by, he told himself. She had plenty of reasons to be sad at the moment, but there was nothing he could do to solve her problems, nothing he could say to ease her fears.

Just walk on by.

Steeling himself, he passed her bedroom. The door was just barely cracked open and the soft sound of her weeping seemed to thunder in his head. It sounded so achingly pitiful.

He got as far as his bedroom door, then stopped. There was no way he could just go to bed with the sound of her crying in his head.

With a reluctant sigh he turned back around, knowing it was foolish, but unable to stop. He paused just outside her door and then knocked softly. "Jane? Are you all right?" He pushed the door open far enough that he could peek into the room, but the room was too dark for him to see her.

"No. I'm not all right."

He heard the rustle of the sheets; then the bedside lamp turned on and there she was, clad in a pale pink nightgown with her hair all tousled around her head and her eyes shiny with tears. She sat up and the sheet fell to her waist, exposing her delicate collarbones above the neckline and the thrust of her breasts against the thin material.

He remained in the doorway, afraid to breathe, afraid to move. She looked so achingly lovely despite her tears.

"What's wrong?" he asked, then grimaced. "Stupid question, right?"

She gave him a watery smile, but it held for only a moment before tears began to trek down her cheeks once again. "I'm being a baby," she said. "I've just been lying here wondering why nobody misses me, why I haven't been reported missing. People are after me and I don't know why and my back hurts so much and I don't have anyone to rub it for me. I'm going to have this baby all alone and I might never know who I am."

He tried to maintain a barrier around his heart. He didn't want to feel her pain, didn't want to get pulled into her despair, but it was impossible not to.

Before he realized what he was doing he found himself standing next to the bed where the sweet scent of her eddied in the air.

"I can't tell you why nobody has missed you, Jane. I can't tell you why you have people after you. But you won't have that baby alone. I'll make sure of that."

Someplace in the back of his mind he knew he was making a promise he didn't intend to keep, but at the moment all he wanted to do was stop her tears, bring that beautiful smile back to her face.

"And if you need somebody to rub your back, then all you need to do is ask," he heard himself saying.

Her lips trembled slightly as she looked up at him. "Would you? Just for a minute or two? I'd appreciate it so much." She scooted over and turned on her side, her back to him and her long, blond hair a spill of shiny strands against the pillow.

He tentatively sat on the side of the bed, his brain screaming that he was making a huge mistake, but his body didn't appear to be listening.

She pulled down the sheet, exposing the length of her, the long nightgown the only barrier between them. He could see the curve of her waist, the flare of her hips and her rounded buttocks as his heartbeat sounded in his ears.

He reached out and laid his palm against her lower back and she released a sigh of sheer pleasure. The warmth of her skin radiated outward through the thin material, and as he began to rub the area, he tried to stay focused on the fact that it was supposed to be a therapeutic massage and nothing more.

"Hmm, that feels so good," she said, her voice a soft whisper.

Lucas didn't reply. He couldn't. His breath was caught in his chest, making speech impossible as desire welled up inside him. He tried to tamp it down, but it refused to dissipate and instead seemed to grow bigger, stronger inside him.

As he rubbed her back with one hand he reached

with the other and touched a strand of her hair. It was luxuriously silky, just as he'd expected. He closed his eyes against a new wave of want.

It's just a back rub, he tried to tell himself. And yet it felt as intimate as anything he'd ever experienced. Her heat, her scent seemed to fill him up. Her tiny mewls of pleasure scorched through him.

His jeans grew tight at his groin as he felt himself responding to her. For God's sake, what was wrong with him? She was pregnant. She didn't even know her name. This whole thing was completely inappropriate. But nothing his brain told him seemed to be making a connection with his body.

He knew he should stop and run from the room, that he was being sucked into a desire greater than any he'd ever felt before. And yet he continued rubbing her back and caressing her hair, trying to tell himself that he was only doing what she needed, not what he wanted.

She moaned and stretched with pleasure. The sound shot a new surge of electricity through his veins. He had to stop, before things spiraled out of control.

Get out, a voice screamed in his head, but he didn't. He couldn't. He was caught…trapped by his own desire to continue.

Instead he worked his hands from her lower back up to the center of her back, then to her shoulders, using just enough pressure to ease but not hurt her tight muscles.

"I can't tell you how good this feels," she said, her voice slightly husky. She turned a bit so that she could look at him, and the curve of her jaw begged for an exploration by his mouth, her lips tormented him as they curved into a soft smile.

"You give a great massage," she said.

He dropped his arms to his sides and stood. "Better?"

The smile fell from her face and she eyed him with an intensity that halted his heart for another long beat. "Better," she replied. She sat up and grabbed his hand. "Don't go, Lucas. Lie here with me and talk for a little while. I don't feel like being alone right now." She patted the bed next to her.

Suddenly he couldn't think of any place he'd rather be than spending a wintry night in bed with her. *No big deal. We're just going to talk,* he told himself.

Still, as he stretched out on the mattress that was still warm with her body heat, he wondered what in the hell he was doing.

IT FELT RIGHT for Lucas to be next to her on the bed. Jane leaned up on one elbow and gazed at him, taking in each and every detail of his features. She loved the length of the lashes that framed his dark eyes and the quirky smile that eased some of the darkness that clung to him. Dark whiskers shadowed the lower half of his jaw and they only added to his rugged, slightly dangerous attractiveness.

"You're staring at me," he said, looking decidedly uncomfortable.

She reached out and placed her palm on his cheek. "I like looking at you," she replied. "You have a nice face, Lucas Washington, but you have the eyes of an old soul."

"Growing up with a father like mine, I guess I aged quickly," he replied. "And if I wasn't a man when I joined the navy, I quickly became one."

She dropped her hand from his face and frowned thoughtfully. "I can't imagine what you went through. Even though I don't have any real specific memories, I think I had a happy childhood."

"I'm glad. I'd like you to have happy memories from your childhood. I can tell you this—you don't have a criminal record of any kind."

She looked at him in surprise. "How do you know that?"

He looked slightly sheepish. "I took a glass you'd used to a buddy of mine who works in the crime lab. He got your fingerprints off the glass and ran it through the system. You weren't in there."

"Why didn't you tell me you did that?"

"I just told you." He smiled. "I didn't want to tell you before I knew the results."

"That's definitely a relief. But what would you have done if I was some sort of criminal?" she asked curiously.

"I guess I would have had to handcuff you and turn you over to my friend Wendall," he replied with a teasing light. "Of course, it's possible you're just a very smart, good criminal and have never been caught."

She moved closer to him, reveling in the scent of him, the warmth of his body radiating out to her. She didn't particularly want to talk. What she wanted was for him to wrap her in his arms. She wanted to feel his lips against hers once again. She wanted to caress his bare skin. She wanted things she shouldn't want, things she was afraid to want.

As she looked at him she forgot what they'd been talking about. All she could think about was how much she wanted a man like Lucas in her life. No, that wasn't true. She wanted Lucas himself in her life. Not just during this time of uncertainty but always.

Of course that was impossible. He'd let her know in every way that he didn't want any kind of lasting relationship. And why would he want a woman carrying another man's child? A woman who was in some kind of trouble?

Still, that didn't stop her from wanting him now. Tomorrow she might wake up with all her memories intact and she'd be on her way back to her former life. But she had tonight. Was it so wrong for her to want to be held, to want to feel loved? "Kiss me, Lucas," she said. "Wrap me up in your arms and kiss me."

His eyes widened and then narrowed. "That's probably not a good idea."

She might have thought he just didn't want to if it wasn't for the pulsing knot in his jaw, the burn in his eyes and the tension in his body.

He wanted her. She felt it radiating from him, saw it spark in the depth of his eyes. She'd heard it in his husky voice.

"I don't care." She reached out and placed her hand on his broad, firm chest. "I know the score, Lucas. I'll probably be out of your life within a matter of days, but that doesn't stop me from wanting to kiss you tonight, right now."

The words were barely out of her mouth as his lips touched hers. Feather-soft, they plied hers with heat. But a soft, gentle kiss wasn't what she wanted. She wanted more. She wanted hard and hot and breathless. She wanted overwhelming and mindless.

She leaned into him, opening her mouth to him, and he responded, swirling his tongue with hers as he pulled her into his arms.

Even with the bulk of her belly, she fit neatly in his arms, as if she belonged, as if she'd never been in another man's arms.

She knew he was aroused. She could tell by his accelerated breathing, by the way his arms tightened around her. His mouth left hers and he trailed kisses down the length of her neck as she ran her hands across his back. She could feel the ridges of his scars and she wanted to kiss them, to somehow caress them away.

Even though she desperately wanted him to make love to her, she knew that wasn't an option. Although she realized sex was usually okay for pregnant women, she'd also heard that in the later stages of pregnancy having sex might induce labor. She didn't want to take that chance, no matter how slim it might be. But she wanted to give him pleasure.

She began to pull up his shirt from the waist, wanting it off, needing to feel his bare skin beneath her fingers. He pulled away from her, and his chest heaved with his rapid breathing. "What are you doing, Jane?" His low, hoarse voice shot a thrill through her.

"I want to love you, Lucas. I want to run my hands across your bare skin. Let me." She touched his shirt. "Take it off and let me love you."

He seemed to freeze, his only movement the rise and fall of his chest as he held her gaze. For a single agonizing moment she thought he was going to spring from the bed and run from the room, from her. But instead he sat up and pulled his shirt over his head and tossed it to the floor.

When he lay back down she placed her face against his chest, loving the warmth of his skin, the rapid beat of his heart beneath her ear. She ran her hands down the length of his chest and he moaned in response.

Her mouth followed her hands, nipping and kissing the heated skin as his hands tangled in her hair. She loved the taste of him, the scent of clean male that clung to him, and when she reached the waist of his jeans she knew she wanted all of him.

Giving pleasure was as exciting, as stimulating as getting it, Jane thought, especially when you were giving it to somebody you cared about.

It didn't take long before Lucas was clad only in his briefs and her caresses and kisses grew more fevered. There was no other thought in her mind but him.

At the moment the past and the future didn't matter. It was just the two of them in the intimacy of the moment. It was she who pulled at his briefs, and when he kicked them off, she wrapped her fingers around his hard length as his mouth found hers in a kiss that seared her to her toes.

She stroked him as he gasped in pleasure against her mouth. She knew that Lucas was a man she'd never forget, that he had etched her heart with an indelible mark that time and circumstance would never erase. And she wanted to be somebody he would never forget.

She felt the rise of his release in his pulsing hardness and moved her hand faster, wanting to take him over the edge, to give him a night with her to remember.

And when he reached the peak, he cried out her name. The only regret she had was that it wasn't really her name, that she might never hear her real name from his lips.

Afterward he got out of bed without a word and

left the room. Instantly, worry rippled through her. Had she offended him with her aggressiveness? Was he angry about what had just happened?

She crept from her bed and went across the hall to the bathroom, heard the sound of running water and realized there must be another bathroom in his master bedroom.

She returned to her bed and lay in the dark, worried about the consequences of what had just happened. Did he think she was terrible? That she was nothing more than a tramp who would fall in bed with anyone?

Moments later he returned to her room, slid back into bed and pulled her into his arms. It was only then she breathed a sigh of relief.

"You realize that was incredibly stupid of us," he finally said.

"It didn't feel stupid," she countered. "It felt wonderful." She raised her head from his chest to look up at him. "Oh, Lucas, you don't have to worry about me expecting more from you than you can give. Everything that has happened to me feels like an out-of-body experience, but I know what just happened between us has nothing to do with real life."

She sighed and dropped her head to his chest once again, where she could hear the solid beat of his heart. "I don't know anything about my past and I certainly can't guess what my future might hold. I just wanted to be with you tonight…a single night in the limbo that has become my life."

He leaned up slightly and turned out the bedside lamp, then tightened his arms around her. "Maybe we'll know more when we confront Charles Blankenship in the morning. For now, get some sleep."

She closed her eyes, and for the first time since all this began, she wasn't afraid. She felt protected and warm with Lucas's arms around her and it took her only minutes to drift off to sleep.

The dream began almost immediately. She was in a church and there were flowers everywhere, filling the interior with sweet fragrance. There was joy in the air and the people in the pews all wore smiles.

Three men stood at the altar, all of them clad in black tuxedos with crisp white shirts and turquoise bowties.

It was a wedding. The groom stood with his back to her and as she gazed at him, her heart filled with happiness. As the traditional wedding march began she started down the aisle, her long, white, silk dress swishing around her legs.

Her heart thudded and she wanted to run to him, to start their life together right now. Lucas, her heart sang, as she stopped herself from running to his side.

Finally she reached where he stood and he turned to look at her, a smile on his handsome face. She froze.

Not Lucas. The man who reached for her hand,

*the groom, was a man she couldn't remember ever
seeing before.*

She woke with a gasp, her heart thundering a
frantic beat. She opened her eyes to the darkness of
the bedroom, aware of Lucas's slow, even breathing
as he slept beside her.

A dream, she told herself. It was nothing more than
a crazy dream. And yet even as she said those words
to herself, she knew the truth. It hadn't been a dream.

It had been a memory.

Chapter Nine

"Anything about the house look familiar?" Lucas asked as he pulled into Charles Blankenship's driveway the next morning. He looked over at Jane, who frowned thoughtfully as she looked at the two-story beige house in front of them.

It was just after ten on another gray, cold day. Breakfast had been awkward. He hadn't been able to get the night before out of his mind.

"No," Jane replied. "It doesn't look familiar at all. I don't think I've ever been here before."

Her hands were clasped tightly in her lap and he could feel her tension. He'd tried to talk her into not coming with him, but she'd been adamant.

"It's my life, Lucas," she'd exclaimed stubbornly, "and if seeing this man in person makes me remember everything, then it's worth any risk."

The problem was Lucas didn't know exactly what risk this might entail. What if Charles Blankenship was some kind of crazy maniac?

They were in his car. Lucas hadn't wanted any-one to get a look at the rental car. He figured Charles had already seen his vehicle, so it made sense to drive it here.

Once again he turned to look at Jane. "When I get out of the car I want you to scoot across and get behind the wheel," he said. "If anything goes wrong, if I get hurt, then I want you to get the hell out of here. Drive back to the safe house and call Micah or Troy."

Her eyes widened and she reached out and grabbed his hand in hers. She squeezed tightly as she held his gaze. "Surely you aren't expecting anything like that?"

"I don't know what to expect," he replied. He pulled his hand from hers. "We don't know what these people are capable of, but I need to know that you'd do exactly what I told you. If anything goes wrong you drive away and don't look back. Promise me, Jane."

He could tell it was a promise she didn't want to make, but as she placed her hands on her stomach and rubbed, she nodded. He knew she would do it for her baby, if not for herself. "I promise," she replied softly.

Lucas opened the car door, and the cold wind slapped his face as he got out of the car. His coat was open, allowing him fast access to his gun if he needed it.

He walked to the front door, then turned to make sure Jane had done as he'd asked. She was in the driver seat, her wide eyes watching him closely.

At least if anything bad happened she'd be able to pull out of the driveway and get the hell out of Dodge. He turned back around and knocked on the door.

This might be a foolish move, but they were stymied, and for the first time since this had all begun he felt like he was playing offense instead of defense.

He knocked once again and the man himself opened the door. Clad in a pair of dress slacks and a long-sleeved white shirt, Charles Blankenship couldn't quite hide the look of surprise that flashed across his blunt features before he schooled them into the curious interest of a stranger. "May I help you?" he asked.

"Yeah, I'd like to know why yesterday evening you chased me through the streets of Kansas City," Lucas said. He didn't intend to waste time playing games with this man.

Charles's gaze shot over Lucas's shoulder to the car, and again a flash of surprise lit his eyes, quickly masked as he looked back at Lucas. "I don't know what you're talking about," he bluffed.

"Oh, I think you do," Lucas replied.

The two men stared at each other for a tense space of time; then Charles sighed and ran a hand through his salt-and-pepper hair. "You cut me off and it made me mad. I'm not proud of my actions. Chalk it up to road rage," he said.

Irritation burned in Lucas's gut. "That wasn't road

rage," he said as he took a step closer to the door. "You were following me. You know the woman in the car?"

"Does she know me?" he countered with a touch of belligerence.

Lucas considered his options. He could tell this man the truth, that Jane didn't have her memories, and see what happened next, or he could bluff. He opted for something in between.

"She hit her head and she's having some memory issues. She doesn't specifically remember you, but she thinks you look familiar. Her memories are coming back every day, and if she remembers that you hurt her, I'll come back here and make you sorry. Got it?"

"There's no need to threaten me," Charles exclaimed.

Lucas offered him a tight smile. "Trust me, that wasn't a threat, that was a promise."

"Look, I don't know that woman, and I already told you I acted badly yesterday. You cut me off and I allowed my anger to take control. It was a simple case of road rage and nothing more. I'm sorry. There, I've apologized. Now get off my porch before I call the police."

"If I see your car anywhere around me, I'll be the one calling the police," Lucas replied as he backed away from the door.

He returned to the car, still watching the door, not willing to turn his back on the man. By the time he reached the car, Jane had scooted back into the passenger seat.

He got in and backed the car out of the drive, a new sense of frustration tying a hard knot in the pit of his stomach.

"I'm not sure exactly what I thought would happen, but this accomplished absolutely nothing," he said as he pulled away, his focus as always divided between the road ahead and the rearview mirror.

Jane reached out and placed her hand on his forearm. Even through the bulk of his coat he could feel her heat, and his irritation grew.

"I'm sorry," she said. "I'm sorry I didn't recognize him."

"You can't do what you can't do," he replied, grateful as she pulled her hand away.

He was also grateful for her silence as they drove back to the safe house. He needed to think, not about what had just transpired with Charles Blankenship, but rather how much longer he could continue to do this, to be responsible for her, to be around her twenty-four hours a day.

The lovemaking of the night before had definitely messed with his mind. Waking up this morning with her spooned against him had been overwhelmingly nice.

Her hair had been a sweet tickle beneath his nose, and the warmth of her body had pressed intimately against his own.

For a few minutes he'd simply remained there, imagining what it would be like to wake up with her every morning for the rest of his life, reluctant to leave her side.

Things were spiraling out of his control. He was spiraling out of control. He was getting too close, wanting things he knew weren't good for him, weren't good for her.

And he wasn't the only one. She was getting in too deep, as well. He felt it in her most simple touch; saw it in her eyes whenever she looked at him; felt it in his heart, in his soul as she'd caressed him the night before.

They couldn't continue this indefinitely. It might take weeks or months for her memory to completely return. There was no way he could do a couple more weeks, let alone a month or two with her. He had to figure out how much longer he was willing to give her and how he was going to tell her that sooner or later he was going to bail.

Once they were back in the house she went to her bedroom to rest and Lucas paced the kitchen, too restless to sit.

The fact that Charles Blankenship had lied to him wasn't surprising. What he'd really hoped was that Jane would see the house or the man and all her memories would come tumbling back.

Charles had lied when he said he didn't know her. He'd lied about everything. Why?

What had happened to her? What had been so terrible that she'd not only run away, but had also shoved the memories of her entire life into the darkest recesses of her mind?

By the time she got up from her nap and joined him in the kitchen, he'd fried burgers and had opened a can of baked beans for dinner. He added a bag of chips to the table and they sat down to eat.

They talked about inconsequential things, the weather, an article in a magazine she was reading, how Kansas City was growing by leaps and bounds.

They didn't talk about men in white vans or all-seeing eye symbols or lost memories. Although the conversation remained pleasant, in the back of his mind Lucas was trying to figure out how to tell her that he was reaching the end of his rope, that it was time they considered going to the authorities for help.

They cleared the table together and a knot of tension formed in his chest when she stood close enough that he could smell her. Memories of the night before stirred in his mind. She'd been soft and warm and giving. She'd been hot and sexy and amazing.

While she'd made love to him last night, it was easy to imagine a time when she would no longer be pregnant and could indulge herself in complete lovemaking.

"You're very quiet this evening," she observed as he put the last plate into the dishwasher. "I did most of the talking during dinner."

"I guess I'm all talked out," he replied. He dried his hands on a hand towel and then turned to look at her.

She must have seen something in his expression, for she leaned against the countertop and released a sigh. "You aren't just talked out, you're Janed out," she said softly. There was not only a whisper of pain in her eyes, but one of fear, as well. "Is this about what happened between us last night?"

"Maybe a little," he said honestly. "Don't get me wrong. It was great…you were great, but it shouldn't have happened."

"I'm glad it did." She lifted her chin as if in defiance. "At least it's one good memory I'll carry with me always."

And so would he, he thought. "It still shouldn't have happened. We don't know what your situation is in your real life, but you know mine. The longer we're together, the more the lines blur between reality and fantasy. I can't be the man in your life, Jane. I don't want to see you get hurt."

"I realize that," she replied, but he thought he heard a touch of wistfulness in her voice. That cinched the deal as far as he was concerned.

He steeled his heart for what he was about to do. "Forty-eight hours, Jane. If you don't get your memory back in forty-eight hours, I'm calling Wendall and we're filing a report."

Once again a dark fear edged into her eyes, but she nodded her head. "All right." She turned and left the kitchen.

Lucas remained standing at the sink, fighting the impulse to run after her and tell her he'd changed his mind.

Forty-eight hours and then she would no longer

be his responsibility. Forty-eight hours and he'd have his life back. What he didn't understand was why the thought didn't fill him with joy.

TWENTY-FOUR HOURS.

The next evening those words whirled around and around in Jane's head, making her alternately sick with fear and beyond sad.

She knew once Lucas turned her over to the police she'd probably never see him again, and that thought ached inside her with a force that was shocking.

She was in love with him. It was as simple and as heartbreaking as that. And when the next twenty-four hours passed she would have to tell him good-bye forever.

As she glanced over at him, her heart swelled and she felt the unwelcome burn of unshed tears. She was on the sofa and he was on the chair nearby, his attention seemingly focused on a crime drama playing on television.

Do not cry, she commanded herself firmly. The last thing she wanted to do was weep and make him feel bad. He'd already gone far above and beyond for her.

She couldn't be hurt or angry with him for wanting to get back to his real life. She couldn't be upset that he didn't love her back enough to want to offer more than he already had.

"I'm going to get something to snack on. You need anything?" he asked when the show ended and he got out of his chair.

Just you, a little voice whispered inside her head. "No, I'm fine. I'm just going to catch a little of the news. Then I'm going to bed." *And tomorrow I'll be gone,* she thought.

As he disappeared into the kitchen she placed her hand on her tummy and wondered what would become of her. Would the police place her in a women's shelter until they could figure out where she belonged? What would happen to her if she never regained her memories?

She focused on the television, her speculation about the future too painful to think about. "More wintry weather ahead," a pert blond newscaster said with a smile. The smile fell and she offered the camera a concerned expression. "A drive-by shooting ends in a young man's death. And police are asking for your help. Have you seen this woman?"

Jane's breath caught in her throat as a picture of her filled the screen. "Lucas," she managed to gasp.

"Details after the break," the blonde said, and a commercial came on.

Lucas appeared in the doorway. "What? What is it?"

She pointed to the television. "It was me. There was a picture of me on the news."

He looked stunned. "What did they say?"

"Details after the break," she replied.

He sank down next to her on the sofa, his attention riveted to the screen. Jane's heart thundered, hurting her chest with the intensity of the beat.

The commercial seemed to last forever, and then

the news returned. The top news story was of a drive-by shooting that had left one teenage boy dead. Jane felt as if she were in agony as she waited for the story that would change everything for her.

There were two more news stories before a picture of her filled the screen. "And now this," the newscaster said. "Concerned family members are looking for this woman. Her name is Julie Montgomery and she's eight months pregnant. She's been missing from her home for the past week. Anyone with any information should call the TIPS hotline." She gave the appropriate number and then they cut away to the weatherman.

Jane sat in stunned silence. Julie. Her name was Julie Montgomery and she had concerned family members looking for her. She rolled the name again and again through her mind. She wasn't sure whether to laugh or cry.

"It suits you," Lucas said softly. "Julie is a nice name."

She turned to look at him. "What happens now?"

"I guess I make a phone call." He pulled his cell phone from his pocket. "You have people who care about you, Julie. It's time you returned to them."

Even though she knew he was right, she was surprised that she didn't feel more relief at the knowledge that she was on her way home— wherever that might be.

"Are you calling the TIPS hotline?" she asked.

"No, I'm calling Wendall. I want to get the name

of the people who reported you missing. Before I turn you over to just anyone, I want them vetted. We need to make sure they're really who they claim to be."

As he stood and punched in numbers on his phone, she thought about what he'd just said. It hadn't occurred to her that it was possible the people who were after her might pose as concerned family members.

She trusted Lucas to see that she wasn't in danger, that the people who were looking for her had only love and concern for her well-being in their hearts.

It was impossible for her to glean any information from Lucas's end of his conversation with Wendall Kincaid. Lucas listened more than talked initially, then spent several minutes telling Wendall about how he'd stumbled upon her and her bout of amnesia.

It seemed to take forever before the men hung up. Lucas set his phone on the coffee table and turned to look at her. "You were reported missing by a Robert Montgomery, who identified himself as your brother-in-law."

"My brother-in-law?" Julie once again placed a hand on her pregnant stomach. She knew there was a man somewhere out there that she'd married. She'd dreamed of him the night after she'd made love to Lucas. She just hadn't told Lucas about that particular memory. "Did he say anything about my husband?" The last word seemed to catch on her tongue.

She had a husband. So why had her brother-in-law reported her missing instead of her husband?

"Wendall only had sketchy information and Robert Mongomery's phone number. Maybe your husband is out of town or in the military. I'll call Robert and set up an initial meeting with him for tomorrow morning. I'll have Troy or Micah sit with you in a car. If Montgomery doesn't come with proof of his relationship to you, then you won't be meeting him at all."

"I'm not sure why I'm so crazy nervous," she said with a small laugh. "This is what we've been waiting for and I know I should be happy, but to be honest, I'm scared."

He reached out and took her hand in his. "That's natural. Even though these people are probably loving relatives, you have no memory of them. We know that there are people after you for some reason or another. It's only normal that you'd feel apprehensive."

She squeezed his hand and leaned against him. She closed her eyes as she drew in the familiar scent of him. He smelled like safety, like passion and home. A lump crept into her throat and again she felt the burn of tears at her eyes.

"I won't see you again after tomorrow, will I?" she asked softly.

"I'm sure we'll run into each other sooner or later," he replied.

They both knew it was a lie, and she loved him even more for pretending that they might maintain some sort of relationship once this was all over.

They remained seated on the sofa for a long time, not speaking, just being with each other. He finally stood and grabbed his cell phone from the coffee table. "First I'm going to call Micah and have him do some digging into Robert Montgomery's life. Then I'm going to make arrangements for the meeting in the morning," he said. "You might as well go on to bed. Get a good night's sleep."

He smiled, but the gesture didn't reach the darkness in his eyes. "Just think, by this time tomorrow night you'll be back where you belong."

She forced a smile to her lips as she stood. "Good night, Lucas," she said. What she couldn't say to him was that she felt in her heart—in her soul—that she belonged with him.

As she headed down the hallway to her bedroom, the tears she'd fought back for the last several minutes began to fall. She should be deliriously happy. She finally knew her name, and tomorrow she'd be reunited with family members, but all she could think about was that after tomorrow she'd never see Lucas again.

Chapter Ten

Micah and Troy were at the safe house at nine the next morning. They all gathered around the table to see what information Micah had managed to dig up on Robert Montgomery.

Lucas couldn't help but notice that Jane's hand trembled slightly as she poured herself a cup of coffee. Julie, he mentally amended. Her name was Julie and he wished there were some way for him to take away her obvious anxiety.

She looked particularly pretty with her hair falling in soft waves around her shoulders and her cheeks flushed with color. She wore the blue blouse he'd picked out for her at the store, and it made her eyes pop.

If all went well he'd be back in his own apartment tonight and Julie Montgomery would only be a fond memory. He tried to summon the joy he'd expected to feel at the idea of getting his life back, but found it curiously absent.

"So, what did you find out about Robert Montgomery?" he asked Micah, determined to focus on the matter at hand and not on matters of his heart.

"He's a forty-four-year-old businessman who owns a lucrative gift shop on Oak Street. He's been married for ten years to a woman named Martha. They live in a small home off North Maple Street. No children, no criminal record for either of them. On paper they look like good, upstanding citizens." He unfolded a sheet of paper and laid it on the table in front of Julie. "Look familiar?"

Lucas could see that it was a copy of a driver's license for Robert Montgomery. The photo depicted a burly man with sandy-colored hair and blue eyes that seemed to jump right off the page.

She studied the photo for a long moment, then shook her head. "No," she replied. "He doesn't look familiar at all, but that doesn't mean anything. I do have amnesia," she added drily.

"Now you want to hear what I dug up about you?" Micah asked.

She sat back in her chair in obvious surprise. "All right." She shoved a strand of hair behind her ear with a shaky hand.

"You're thirty years old and you worked as an elementary school teacher until two years ago when you married David Montgomery, Robert's younger brother." He paused a moment as if to give her time to digest the information.

"Third grade," she said with a touch of surprise

in her voice. She paused a moment, then nodded and smiled. "Yes, I taught third grade." The smile wavered as she continued to look at Micah. "Where's my husband?"

"Dead. I'm sorry, Julie. Your husband was killed almost eight months ago during a mugging," Micah said softly.

Lucas's heart fell at this bit of information. So, there was no loving husband for her to return to. She was alone just as she'd felt she was despite having no real memories.

She sighed and nodded once again as her hands lowered to her stomach. "Somehow I knew it." She turned to look at Lucas. "I told you I thought I had been alone before all this happened."

"You own a home near Robert and Martha's house," Micah continued. "But after your husband's death you apparently moved in with them and put the house up for sale." Micah leaned back in his chair. "That's all I could get in the short amount of time I had."

"At least I know more now than I did when I woke up this morning. Thank you," she said.

"So, how are you going to work this?" Troy asked.

Lucas looked at his watch. "In thirty minutes I'm meeting Robert and his wife at the Calico Café. I told him last night on the phone to bring proof of his relationship to Julie, pictures and documents or whatever he had. I explained to him that she was having some memory problems. I'd like you and Micah to stay with Julie in one of your cars until I feel comfortable that it's okay for her to enter the restaurant. Then I'll call one of you on your cell and you can bring her in to meet her family."

He turned to gaze at Julie. Her anxiety was through the roof. Her lower lip trembled slightly and he wanted nothing more than to cover it with his own, hold her until her trembling halted. "It's going to be okay, Julie. It's time for you to be with people who care about you, people who will watch over you."

He hesitated a moment, then added, "If you feel alarmed, then you don't have to go with them. We'll bring you back here." He told himself that was the last thing he wanted, that it would be best for everyone involved if she returned to her rightful place.

"Thank you," she replied. "I'm sure it's all going to work out just fine." She raised her chin a notch, and at that moment Lucas thought she was one of the bravest women he would ever know.

"Then we should get out of here," Troy said.

They all rose from the table and went into the living room, where they grabbed their coats. Julie went down the hallway to the bedroom where she'd been staying and returned a few seconds later with the small black overnight bag packed with everything she had.

"I'm ready," she said with a lift of her chin despite the tremor in her voice.

Minutes later they were on the road, Lucas in his rental car followed by the others in Micah's car. As he drove, Lucas's mind filled with the sound of Julie's laughter, the pleasure of morning coffee with her bright smile across from him at the table.

The taste of her filled his mouth, and the scent of her seemed to ride the air. A wave of sadness suffused him, shocking him with its heavy weight.

He could have loved her if he was a loving kind of man. *Which I'm not,* he reminded himself. He could never be the man she wanted, the man she needed. He reached up and touched the scar on the back of his neck to remind himself of where he'd come from. She and her baby were much better off without him.

Surely her extended family would take care of her, see that both she and the baby were happy and healthy. He had to believe that. And eventually she'd find some special man to share her life with her, the kind of man she deserved.

Lucas turned into the parking lot of the café as Micah drove on by. He would park someplace up the street until Lucas called him to bring Julie.

He found a parking space near the front door and got out of the car. The wind seemed colder, but it was also filled with the scent of bacon, eggs and strong coffee.

As he entered, a quick glance at the diners told him that Montgomery hadn't arrived yet. He took a booth next to a window with a view of the parking lot and ordered a cup of coffee from the waitress. He might have ordered a full breakfast if his stomach hadn't been so tied in knots.

When the coffee arrived he wrapped his fingers around the mug and told himself once again that this was a happy occasion. It was what they'd been seeking—Julie's identity and the place where she belonged.

He'd only been sitting for about five minutes when he saw a beige sedan pull in and Robert Montgomery get out of the driver's side. An attractive woman with dark hair got out of the passenger side and together they headed toward the café.

This was it. The moment Lucas had wished for, the chance to get rid of Julie once and for all and get back to his own life. No more safe house, no more intimate breakfasts or back rubs that went too far.

As Robert and Martha stepped inside, their gazes swept the area. Lucas raised a hand to motion them over as he stood.

"Lucas Washington?" Robert had the deep, rich, booming voice of a radio personality.

Lucas nodded and the two men shook hands. Robert introduced his wife and then they all sat back down in the booth. Robert placed a manila folder in front of him.

"Where's Julie?" Martha asked, her gaze darting around the room.

"I wanted to meet the two of you first," Lucas said. The waitress arrived at the table and both

Robert and Martha ordered coffee. When the coffee was served, Lucas explained to them how he'd found Julie and about her amnesia.

"Oh my goodness," Martha exclaimed when Lucas had finished his story. "That poor girl. She's all right? The baby is all right?"

"Physically she's fine, but she's still struggling with some memory issues," Lucas replied. "Which is why I asked you to bring proof of your relationship to her. Since she can't remember you, I want to make sure you're who you really say you are."

"Of course," Robert said. He opened the folder in front of him and handed Lucas a photo. It was a wedding picture. Julie was the bride, a handsome blond man was the groom and on either side of them were Robert and Martha. "That was the day my brother married Julie," he said. "We were thrilled that he'd found such a lovely woman to share his life with, and we were eager to welcome her into our family."

She was a beautiful bride, Lucas thought as he studied the picture. And a little over a year after this happy photo had been taken she had become a pregnant widow. He handed the photo back to Robert.

"It's been almost ten days. Why didn't you report her missing sooner?" he asked. Micah had told him that according to the neighbors Julie was living in Martha and Robert's home. Why had it taken so long for them to realize she wasn't there?

"She told us she felt like she wanted some time

alone, that she was going to stay at her house for a few days," Robert explained. "We thought maybe she just needed some space. Our home isn't huge, and we were kind of on top of each other." He frowned. "She doesn't remember any of this?"

"No," Lucas replied. There was absolutely no reason for him not to trust the two people in front of him, but he couldn't explain the faint thrum of apprehension that worried him.

Maybe it was nothing more than the fact that he hated the idea of Julie leaving. Or perhaps it was the knowledge that she had no husband, no father for the baby she carried.

This was definitely more difficult than he'd thought it would be. He hadn't expected that handing her over and telling her goodbye would feel like a loss.

JULIE NEARLY CAME UNGLUED when Micah's cell phone rang. The last thirty minutes had been the most agonizing she thought she'd ever spend.

She leaned over the back of the front seat as Micah answered. When he clicked off, he looked at her in the rearview mirror. "Buckle up, it's a go."

So, Robert Montgomery had passed the Lucas test and she was about to be reintroduced to family members whom she'd been close to before whatever event had stolen her memories.

She leaned back and fastened her seat belt as Micah pulled away from the curb where they had been parked and headed toward the café.

"You okay?" Troy asked.

"Nervous, but okay," she replied. Her heart felt as if it might pound right out of her chest and the baby did a sudden somersault as if sensing her anxiety.

"You know Lucas would never put you in a dangerous situation. Both Micah and I can tell that he cares about you."

Troy's words created a ring of pain around her heart. He might care about her, but not enough to want to be a part of her life. Once her picture had appeared on the evening news he'd certainly wasted no time arranging to get rid of her.

She frowned. That wasn't fair. Lucas believed he was doing what was best for her, and even though it pained her, she knew she had to somehow push him out of her heart.

As Micah pulled up in front of the café, Troy got out to escort her inside. She grabbed her overnight bag from the seat next to her in one hand and grabbed his arm with the other.

She was so nervous her legs felt wobbly beneath her. Maybe she'd take one look at Robert and Martha and all her memories would instantly return. She wanted that. Even though they'd found out her name and knew bits and pieces of her life, she wanted, needed her memories back.

As they entered the café she immediately spied Lucas. Martha Montgomery rose as Julie approached the booth, and when Julie got close enough the older woman pulled her into a hug.

"Oh, Julie, dear. We've been worried sick about you," she exclaimed.

Julie held herself stiffly in the stranger's arms, but as the hug continued she felt herself begin to relax. They weren't strangers…they were family, she reminded herself.

As Martha released her, Julie slid into the booth next to Lucas, surprised to discover that Troy had disappeared.

"Julie, honey, we know this is difficult for you," Robert said. "Lucas has explained about your memory issues. But I'm sure once we get you home, you'll be just fine. The baby's crib is all set up and we're eager to get you settled back in where you belong."

"Before that happens, there's something you should know," Lucas said. "Somebody tried to grab Julie and shove her in the back of a van at the store the other day. You have any clue why that might have happened?"

Martha and Robert exchanged pointed glances as Julie felt a new tension coil in her stomach. "My brother, God rest his soul, was a good, but troubled man," Robert said. "He had a weakness for drugs and gambling. At the time of his death, he owed money to people who don't easily overlook debts." He turned his attention from Lucas to Julie. "Part of the reason we had you move in with us was that you had been receiving threatening phone calls from these people. I guess they got tired of making phone calls and decided to get more aggressive."

Julie looked down at the table as she tried to process this new information. Her husband had been a drug abuser and a gambler? She could only guess that the marriage hadn't been a happy one. Was that why she'd forgotten it, forgotten David?

"The problem," Robert continued, "is that Julie doesn't have any money. Another reason we decided to move her in with us was so we could sell her house and get her out from under that payment. Our plan was for her to live with us until the baby was born, and then she could go back to teaching and get on her feet."

"There was no life insurance policy on her husband?" Lucas asked.

Robert grimaced. "My brother cashed it in months before his death. He left Julie nothing."

"Why don't we order some breakfast and chitchat a bit about more pleasant things?" Martha suggested.

Julie was grateful for the suggestion. Hopefully it would give her a little more time to feel comfortable with the people who intended to take her home with them.

Lucas motioned for the waitress and they all ordered. While they ate, Robert and Martha told her a little more about her life with them.

With each moment that passed, a weary acceptance filled Julie. Robert and Martha appeared to be kind, well-meaning people. There was no reason for her not to leave with them.

Except that she didn't want to leave the man

seated next to her. Lucas was quiet during the meal, as if he'd already disconnected from the situation, from her.

Love me, her heart wanted to plead. Ask me to stay with you. Don't send me away with people I don't remember. Don't send me away at all. But all too quickly they had finished eating and it was time for her to leave.

There was nothing to stop her from going with them. They'd had the documentation to prove that they were who they claimed to be, and Julie knew it was time for her to get back to whatever life she'd forgotten.

As they reached the sidewalk outside, Robert and Martha started toward their car as Lucas grabbed Julie's arm. "She'll be right there," he said, indicating they should go on.

She looked up at him, wishing for things he couldn't give, yearning for an ending different than the one she was getting. "They seem like really nice people," she finally said.

He nodded, his gaze intent on her, and for just a moment she thought she saw something wonderful in the depths of his eyes, something warm and caring, something that looked like love. "You're going to be just fine, Julie." He said the words forcefully, as if trying to convince himself as well as her. He reached up and tenderly tucked a strand of her hair behind her ears, then stepped back from her.

"So I guess this is goodbye." Her throat grew

thick with emotion. She finally felt free to say the words that burned in her heart.

His strong jaw clenched and his eyes darkened. "I know through this whole thing I've been your lifeline, but once you get your memories back you'll realize what you feel for me is nothing more than gratitude."

Was he right? Did she feel so strongly about him because she was lost in a sea of the unknown? Was the love she felt for him nothing more than gratitude masquerading as something deeper?

"Julie, I told you not to want anything from me, that I'm not cut out to be a husband or a father."

"I know. I just don't understand why you'd say that about yourself. You have all the qualities it takes to be a wonderful husband and father." She wanted to touch him, but his eyes grew even darker and he took another step back from her.

"You have my cell phone number if you need anything. Goodbye, Julie." He shoved his hands in his coat pockets, a distinct dismissal of her, of any hopes she might have had to the contrary.

"Goodbye, Lucas," she replied. She tightened her grip on her overnight bag, then turned and headed toward Martha and Robert's car.

Her heart sat like a heavy boulder in her chest. Robert opened the back door of his car with a reassuring smile and she slid in. As he pulled out of the parking lot, she turned and gazed back at Lucas, who hadn't moved from his position on the sidewalk.

Her last impression of him was that he looked as alone as she felt, and that somehow this was wrong, all wrong.

"I'm sure you're exhausted from all this drama," Martha said. "All of this can't be good for the baby. We're going to make sure you get plenty of rest and healthy meals."

Julie offered her a weak smile. "I am tired," she admitted. But not from anything other than the difficulty in telling Lucas goodbye.

She stared out the window and watched the passing scenery, her thoughts still on the man she'd just left. There was no way she believed that her feelings for him were mere gratitude. She knew what she felt in her heart, and it was love.

"Are you warm enough back there?" Robert's voice pulled her from her thoughts.

She met his piercing blue gaze in the rearview mirror. "I'm fine," she assured him. Fine. Everyone seemed to be using that word a lot when it came to her and her future. You're going to be just fine, Lucas had told her. But she didn't feel as if she'd ever be completely fine again.

She sat up straighter and frowned as she noticed they were driving north. She could have sworn Robert and Martha lived south of the café where they had met.

"Are we going home?" she asked, a strange feeling of dread welling up inside her.

"We're taking you right where you belong, dear," Martha said.

Julie's sense of dread grew bigger, a faint alarm ringing in the back of her head. Then she saw it just ahead of them—the Church of Enlightenment. Even though she couldn't remember coming here, didn't recognize it from memory, she knew what it was.

"What are we doing here?" she asked. She unfastened her seat belt as Robert pulled the car up to the gate that led into the inner compound.

He clicked a remote button on his dash and the gate opened. At the same time Julie tried to open the back car door, somehow knowing that she needed to escape.

But the door wouldn't open. Panic welled up inside her. Why was she locked in like a prisoner? Why were they bringing her here? Oh God, something was wrong. Something was terribly wrong.

As Robert pulled through the gate and it clunked shut behind them, Julie's memories came rushing back. And with them came the knowledge that she was in grave danger.

Chapter Eleven

Lucas watched them pull out of the café parking lot as his heart twisted in a way he'd never felt before. She was better off without him. Robert and Martha Montgomery seemed like fine people, and eventually Julie would find another man, one who would be a great husband and a terrific father. She was better off without him, and he was better off without her.

Even as he told himself this, he hurried to his car and got in, driven by an impulse he didn't understand. He wanted to see the house where she'd live, the place where she'd bring her baby after he was born and get on with her life.

He drove several car lengths behind them, not wanting her to see him. He didn't want her to think that he was coming after her, that he'd changed his mind and wanted to take her home with him.

It didn't take long for him to be confused by the direction they were traveling, and with his confusion came a spark of concern.

The farther north they drove, the more concern Lucas felt, and when the Church of Enlightenment came into view, the concern transformed to a screaming alarm.

He stepped on the gas in an effort to catch up to them, but before he could, their car disappeared behind the security gates. He braked and stared at the seemingly impenetrable gate that surrounded the buildings within.

Why had they brought her here? During their conversation nobody had mentioned the church. Julie had been terrified by the symbol of the all-seeing eye that the church used as its emblem. Why would they have brought her here? What did they— what did Julie have to do with the church?

He ran the conversation they'd shared over breakfast through his head again and again, seeking something he'd missed, a clue he'd somehow overlooked.

In retrospect the only thing that sounded odd was the idea that goons would be after Julie because of her husband's drug and gambling debts. Julie had no money. The goons would have nothing to gain by going after her, and they sure wouldn't try to grab her in the middle of the day in a busy parking lot.

She was in trouble. He'd handed her right over to danger. He slammed the steering wheel with the palms of his hands, then grabbed his cell phone from his pocket and called Chief Kincaid. Wendall answered on the second ring.

"Wendall, it's Lucas. I need your help."

"What's up?"

"Can you meet me in fifteen minutes in front of the Church of Enlightenment?"

Wendall must have heard the thrum of urgency in Lucas's voice, for he didn't ask any questions. "I'll be there."

"And Wendall, could you bring a couple of officers with you?"

There was a momentary pause. "Are you in danger?"

"No, but I think somebody else is," Lucas replied.

"On my way."

Lucas dropped his cell phone on the seat next to him and backed away from the security gate. Instead he pulled to park in front of the church, his heart pounding with a nauseating intensity.

Why was she here? It didn't make sense. He glanced at his watch. He felt as if each minute that passed was an hour as he waited for reinforcements to arrive.

What he wanted was to talk to Julie, to assure himself that she was okay. He'd like to storm the fence, either ram his car through it or climb over it. But he knew that if he was arrested for destruction of personal property or trespassing, he wouldn't be any help at all to Julie. *If she needs help,* he reminded himself.

He supposed it was possible the Montgomerys had brought her here to visit a friend, or to worship before taking her home. He tried to convince himself that those scenarios were possible, but he remained unconvinced.

Once again he checked his watch. God, could the minutes move any slower? With nervous energy screaming through him, he unfastened his coat and placed a hand on the butt of his gun.

He'd kill for her.

The thought shocked him. As a navy SEAL he'd killed before, but that had been war, cases of kill or be killed. It wasn't something he'd enjoyed, nor had he ever expected to do it again in civilian life.

But for Julie and her unborn son, he'd do whatever it took to protect her, even if it meant killing again.

He breathed a sigh of relief as a patrol car pulled in beside him and Wendall got out. Wendall Kincaid was good-looking, dark-haired and the youngest and most popular chief of police in Kansas City's history.

Although he frowned on some of Recovery Inc.'s methods, he'd become a friend to all three of the men. "What have we got?" he asked.

As Lucas began to fill him in on what was going on, he saw a frown etched deeper and deeper into Wendall's forehead.

"What do you want from me, Lucas?" Wendall asked when Lucas was finished explaining everything. "Julie is a consenting adult and she went willingly with these relatives of hers. There isn't much I can do about that."

"But they told me they were taking her home," he protested.

Wendall shrugged. "So they had a change of plans. No crime has occurred here."

Lucas grabbed Wendall by the shoulder. "Maybe not yet, but I'm telling you this isn't right. Julie would never have willingly come here. Just check it out. Make them bring her out here to talk to me. If she tells me this is where she wants to be, then I'll walk away and not bother her, not bother you again."

Wendall frowned once again. "Let's go check it out," he said.

Lucas dropped his hand from Wendall's shoulder and breathed a sigh of relief. "Thanks, man. I won't forget this."

Minutes later Lucas, Wendall and Officer Ben Branigan approached the locked gate. It was Wendall who found a buzzer that Lucas hadn't noticed before. He rang it and a moment later a man's voice replied. "This is private property, please state your business."

"This is Chief of Police Wendall Kincaid. I'd like to speak with Robert Montgomery," Wendall said in a voice that rang with his authority.

Lucas's chest was filled with such a cold, hard knot that he found breathing difficult. He told himself to relax, but it wasn't happening, wouldn't happen until he knew with a gut certainty that Julie was okay.

The resulting silence seemed to last a lifetime, but finally Robert's deep, familiar voice boomed out of the hidden speaker.

"What can I do for you?"

"I want to talk to Julie," Lucas shouted over Wendall's shoulder.

"I'm afraid, Mr. Washington, that Julie doesn't wish to speak with you," Robert replied smoothly.

"I really must insist that we see Julie," Wendall said.

Once again his words were met with a long silence. Lucas could feel his heartbeat not only in his chest, but banging at his temples. Was it possible that she didn't want to see him? That he'd hurt her by sending her off where she was supposed to belong, even though hurting her was the last thing he'd wanted to happen?

"There's nothing wrong with Julie except that she's stressed and wants some peace and quiet. I see you have an officer with you," Robert said. "I'll allow him to come in and speak with Julie. Perhaps he can convince her to come out and talk to you, but I won't force her to do anything she doesn't want to do."

Wendall looked at Lucas, who in turn looked at Officer Branigan. He shrugged. "I'll go in and talk to her," he said. "I don't have a problem with it."

"Okay," Wendall said into the speaker. "Officer Branigan will come in and speak with Julie."

Minutes later a tall, burly man approached the gate from the inside. He offered them a friendly smile, as if it was business as usual to have the chief of police standing at the gate.

"Officer Branigan? You can come on in." He opened the gate and allowed the cop inside, then closed and locked the gate once again.

Branigan turned and offered Wendall and Lucas

a thumbs-up signal. Lucas tried to tell himself that surely if anything was wrong the people inside wouldn't want an armed cop in their midst.

Lucas looked at Wendall, "Don't you think it's damned suspicious that they wouldn't let us in?"

"Maybe," Wendall agreed. "But I have no jurisdiction to just barge in. At least they allowed an officer in to speak with him."

Still, Lucas couldn't get rid of the feeling that Julie was in some kind of terrible danger and needed his help.

JULIE SAT ON THE EDGE of the bed in an attractive bedroom with an adjoining bath. Under other circumstances she might have appreciated the fine mahogany furniture and the beautiful tapestries that hung on the walls.

But as beautiful as the bedroom was, it was nothing more than her prison. And it had been her prison for a month before Lucas had found her shivering in the back of that car.

She remembered everything now, her marriage to David, his unexpected death and the fact that her brother and sister-in-law were monsters.

Robert was the prophet, the father figure behind the curtain who preached in anonymity on Sundays to a congregation who desperately wanted to believe in something different than what traditional religion offered.

More than anything, she remembered that they

wanted her baby. She wrapped her arms around her belly and looked around the room for the hundredth time since being locked inside.

The room was located on the third floor. Although there were two windows, there was no way she could chance jumping. She would probably kill herself. But more importantly she could hurt her baby.

There was nothing to use as a weapon, no way for her to fight the people who held her captive. She squeezed her eyes closed tightly against the tears that threatened to fall. She refused to cry and she refused to think about Lucas, knowing if she did she would start crying and never stop.

Her husband, David, was dead. That much had been true. He'd been the victim of a mugger who had stabbed him to death. And Robert and Martha *had* taken her into their home days after the funeral.

Over the next couple of months, things had been going okay.

Robert and Martha had embraced her and her unborn child with love and support—or so she'd thought. David had told her when they'd married that Robert couldn't have children of his own, that a childhood illness had left him sterile. Both Martha and Robert had seemed to have made peace with the fact that they would never have children.

It had been at the beginning of her seventh month of pregnancy that everything had changed. She'd started talking to Martha about the possibility of moving to a new town. Maybe in another state after the baby was born. She wanted a fresh start. She'd been brought here and held prisoner. Robert had told her his plan for her and her child.

She jumped to her feet as the door opened and Robert walked in, along with a uniformed police officer. The sight of the officer should have produced a sense of relief in her, but instead it stirred a new fear.

She'd seen him before. Here, in her prison. He was a member of Robert's wicked board, a man seeking wealth and power and definitely not on the side of law and order.

"We have a little problem," Robert said. "It seems your boyfriend has brought the chief of police to check on your welfare."

Lucas was here? Oh, thank God, he'd come for her. Her heart swelled with hope. "Just let me go, Robert. I won't say anything to anyone. I won't press any charges against you. Just let me go and you'll never hear from me again."

Robert smiled at her indulgently. "I've worked too hard, too long to do that, Julie. The child you carry will be mine. He will herald in a new world for the Church of Enlightenment. He will be the new Prophet and offer hope to all."

"Why don't you tell the truth, Robert?" she said angrily. "This isn't about the church and hope. It's about money and power."

Robert's smile grew. "There is that," he agreed. "It's amazing how much money people will cough up if they think it means their salvation. For the new prophet they'll give up their property, their retirement funds. We'll build our own little community here with people working for the church and we'll all get wealthy. Right, Ben?"

The police officer nodded. "Can't get wealthy working for the man," he replied.

"You'll burn in hell," Julie exclaimed.

"Perhaps," Robert agreed easily. "But what a life I'm planning before I die. The best of everything for the new prophet's father on earth." His smile fell and his blue eyes grew icy. "But before any of this can happen we have the little problem of your Romeo and his friend at our gates."

"I have a feeling they aren't going away until they see that she's okay in person," Ben said. "She needs to tell them everything is all right."

"And I'm not about to do that," Julie replied fervently. *Lucas,* her heart cried. *Please save me from this nightmare.*

"I think you will," Robert countered confidently. "I think you're going to go down to the gate and tell them that you have all your memories back and this is where you want to be."

"And why would I do that?" she demanded.

Robert reached into his pocket and pulled out a photo and held it out to her. Reluctantly she took it from him and gasped in alarm.

It was a picture of Loretta, taken as she was entering the hospital where she worked. "We can get her anywhere, anytime we want. Same with your boyfriend. Neither of them will know who to fear. They'll never see us coming. If you don't cooperate with us, Loretta Washington is a dead woman. And after we kill her, we'll get Lucas. We would have taken you sooner from Loretta's apartment, but as we made our plans, you disappeared. Besides, it's much better this way. We don't need any police problems."

A dull roar resounded in Julie's head. She believed him. She believed every word he said. They would find Loretta and they would kill her, and eventually they'd get to Lucas, too.

She held both Loretta's and Lucas's lives in her hands and there was no way she could sacrifice them for herself. They had both been so kind to her, a stranger in need and she wouldn't reward their kindness by placing them at risk.

"All right," she finally said, then grimaced. "I'll do whatever you tell me to do, just leave them alone."

Robert took the picture of Loretta from her and tucked it back in his shirt pocket. "I thought you'd see things my way." He grabbed her by the arm, making her skin crawl with his touch. "Just keep in mind, if you screw up, you're putting a bullet in their heads. Make this problem go away, Julie."

As he led her out of the room, Julie's heartbeat was a dull throb in her chest. There would be no magical rescue for her. She was going to have her baby here and she had no doubt that Robert would see to it that she didn't survive the birth.

As they walked down the long hallway that led to the stairs, she remembered the hall from her nightmares. She'd run this way on the night she'd escaped.

As she slowly walked between Robert and Ben, she remembered that night. She'd been told of Robert's plot for her baby, and when Gemma Walker, the old woman who brought her meals, had come in to serve her dinner that night, she'd shoved past her.

Gemma had hit her on the head with the serving tray, resulting in the wound on her forehead, but Julie had managed to slip by her. That night she'd gotten out of the house, and through some amazing good luck had found the security gate unlocked.

She wouldn't get a chance for escape again. They reached the front door of the house, but before they walked outside Robert provided a coat for her and himself.

It didn't matter to her whether she wore a coat out into the cold afternoon or not. No cotton or nylon fabric could warm the icy core inside her.

As they left the house and walked across the long expanse of concrete toward the security gate, Robert squeezed her arm. "It's in everyone's best interest for you to look happy."

She gave an imperceptible nod. He didn't have to tell her what needed to be done, she knew. Still, the minute she saw Lucas at the gate, it took every ounce of her self-control to keep herself from crying out for him, to keep from launching herself over the gate and into his arms.

Instead, as Robert released his hold on her arm she summoned all the inner strength she could find to get through the next few minutes.

"Julie." Lucas's voice was filled with raw concern as he took a step toward her. The tall, dark-haired man standing beside him held him back.

"Julie, I'm Chief of Police Wendall Kincaid," he said. "Lucas here seems to think you're in some sort of trouble."

Her heart was a sick thud in her chest as she pasted on a bright smile. "In trouble?" She looked at Lucas. "No, I'm not in trouble. In fact, everything is better than it's been in days. Lucas, I've got my memories back. It was amazing. The minute we pulled through the gates here, they all came tumbling back to me."

Lucas's eyes were filled with doubt as he stared at her intently. "And you want to be here?"

"I'm safe here, Lucas," she replied, relieved that her voice didn't tremble, didn't waver, but sounded strong and normal. "Martha and Robert brought me here to keep me safe from the men who are after me because of David's debts."

"Really, Mr. Washington, you're looking for drama where there is none," Robert said smoothly.

"Lucas, I really appreciate everything you did for me," Julie said. "But I'm fine now." She hoped the smile that curved her lips didn't look as plastic as it felt.

Wendall looked at Lucas, who still stared at her with an intensity that made her heart ache. "And this is where you want to be?" Lucas asked.

"Absolutely," she replied; then she reached a hand up and deliberately tugged on the end of her hair.

"Are we done here?" Robert asked with a touch of impatience. "It's cold and Julie is weary." He placed an arm around her shoulder and she fought the shiver of revulsion that tried to take hold of her at his touch.

"I guess we're done," Lucas said flatly. "Sorry to bother you all. Julie, I hope things go well for you." He turned and headed back to his car, followed by Wendall and Ben.

"You did very well, my dear," Robert said as he guided her back toward the house.

Julie barely heard him as she felt the last of her hope flutter away. She'd tried to tell Lucas that she was lying by the tug of her hair, but obviously he hadn't gotten it.

She glanced backward just before she went back into the house and saw Lucas's car driving away. It was over, done, and she was helpless to fight Robert and his minions.

She hadn't been able to save herself, but at least she'd saved Lucas and his sister. Still, as Robert led her back up the stairs to her room, she began to weep for Lucas, for her baby and for herself.

Chapter Twelve

She'd lied.

When she had said she was fine and where she wanted to be, she'd been lying. She'd definitely pulled on the ends of her hair when she'd said those words.

"My mother said she could always tell when I was fibbing because I'd tug on the end of my hair." Julie's words reverberated around and around in his head. She'd been trying to signal him, to let him know that she was in trouble.

Lucas hadn't even gone half a block from the church when he pulled out his cell phone and punched in a number. "Meet me at my place in fifteen minutes," he said to Micah.

"What's going on?"

"I'll tell you when you get there. And call Troy. I want him there, too."

Lucas hung up, tossed the phone on the seat next to him and stepped on the gas pedal, eager to get to his apartment and plan a course of action.

He knew there was no point in talking to Wendall. Julie was a consenting adult. She'd told them all that she wanted to be in the compound behind the church. Without any more evidence to the contrary, Wendall's hands would be tied.

Besides, going through legal channels for help could take days, and even then he'd have to convince Wendall that a pull on the hair had been a signal instead of a simple gesture.

But Lucas wasn't bound by law. He'd seen all the evidence he needed to see in the simple tug of her hair. Rage balled up in his chest as he thought of Julie afraid and alone with people who meant her and her unborn baby harm.

He still didn't understand what they wanted with her, why they would take her to the compound and hold her there against her will, but he didn't need a reason to go in and get her out.

He also didn't know if she'd lied about having her memories back or not. But it didn't matter. Nothing mattered except getting her out of that place and away from those people. Guilt ripped through him. He'd handed her over to them. He'd sent her back into danger.

It was almost two in the afternoon by the time he reached his apartment. Micah and Troy were already in the parking lot awaiting his arrival.

They didn't speak until they were in the apartment and then Lucas told them what had transpired at the church compound.

"I don't know what's going on there. I don't know why they're holding her, but we have to get her out," he said. "I know she's in danger." He thumped his chest with his fist. "I feel it here."

He was grateful that neither of his friends tried to dissuade him from his belief. In any case it would have been a waste of time. With or without them, Lucas intended to get Julie out.

"What do you have in mind?" Micah asked as he leaned forward in his chair at the kitchen table. His eyes glittered with the call to war. There was nothing Micah and Troy enjoyed more than action.

"A covert operation," Lucas replied. "We go in under the cover of night and we don't come out unless we have her with us."

Micah sat back and frowned thoughtfully. "What do you know about the house where she's being held?"

"Not much. It's a three-story mansion. I don't know how many people are inside. I don't know if she's being held under armed guard. I'm not sure what we'd be walking into."

Troy smiled. "Wouldn't be the first time," he replied.

"I'll see if I can get a copy of permits and maybe a floor plan of the place this afternoon," Micah said.

"And I'll do a little reconnaissance work and see if I can tell how many people might be inside and whether they're armed or not," Troy added.

Lucas nodded, gratitude swelling in his chest.

"Why don't we coordinate back here at seven tonight and make final plans?"

Troy and Micah left immediately, and Lucas paced the confines of his kitchen, his thoughts filled with Julie. It was only now that he recognized the depths of his feelings for her.

He loved her.

He'd never allowed himself to fall in love with any woman, but somehow Julie had gotten under his defenses, touched places in his heart that had never been touched before.

He had no illusions. There was no happily ever after for them. His loving Julie didn't magically absolve him of the issues that would forever keep him a solitary man.

But he wanted her safe. He wanted her healthy. And eventually he hoped she'd be happy. He knew in his gut that none of those things were going to happen as long as she was in that house. He had to get her out and then he could walk away from her with no regrets.

The late afternoon and early evening hours crept by with agonizing slowness. Lucas got on his computer and tried to find out everything he could about the Church of Enlightenment, seeking answers to questions he didn't even know how to pose.

He did a Google search of the names of the few people he knew from the church—Charles Blankenship, Robert Montgomery, Martha Montgomery and of course, Julie. Charles Blankenship had a Web site devoted to his family with nothing inflammatory or unusual about it. He could find nothing on Robert and Martha except a special interest article in a local newspaper about Robert's gift shop.

He found the article about David's murder. It had occurred as the man had left an ATM. The case was never solved. His obituary mentioned that he was survived by his older brother, Robert, and his wife, Julie, but Lucas already knew that.

All in all, the computer time was a bust and once again Lucas took to pacing the kitchen, his head whirling with crazy thoughts and emotions he'd never felt before.

By the time seven o'clock arrived, Lucas was like a cat on a hot tin roof, filled with a nervous energy that begged to be directed into action.

He changed his clothes, opting for a pair of black jeans and a long-sleeved black turtleneck that would allow him to blend into the night.

When Troy and Micah arrived they were dressed similarly, and they didn't come empty-handed. They brought stun guns, rope and grappling hooks for rappelling. More importantly, they brought their stealth and clandestine methods and expertise as ex–navy SEALs at getting in and out without detection.

For the next four hours they plotted and planned. Micah had somehow gotten hold of a floor plan of the house, and they speculated in what room Julie might be held.

Troy had counted eight men going in and out of the house who he thought might be armed. But why would a church-owned establishment need armed guards?

By midnight they were all champing at the bit, ready to take on an entire army to save one beautiful pregnant woman. It was decided that they would park their cars a mile away near the fields that served as a backyard to the home. There they would scale a tall chain-link fence.

They would spread out and each find a way into the house. There was no need to plan the specifics, each would do whatever necessary to gain entrance. The goal was to get in and out without encountering anyone, but if they did, they each knew how to take out a threat without making a sound.

They would go in at twelve-thirty and hopefully rendezvous back at the safe house with Julie in hand by one-thirty.

"I just want to tell you both how much I appreciate this," Lucas said as they left his apartment. None of them had spoken of the fact that before the night was over there was a possibility they could be in jail—or dead.

Troy clapped Lucas on the back. "In until the end," he said.

It was what they'd said when they'd served side by side, and in that moment Lucas realized how rich his life was in having these two men as friends.

They left Lucas's apartment complex, each in his

own vehicle, and within minutes were in position about a mile away from the compound.

None of them spoke as they ran toward their objective.

They scaled the fence that thankfully wasn't electrified. The minute they split apart and Troy and Micah disappeared into the darkness of the night, Lucas's thoughts were solely on Julie.

Was she still okay? Had they harmed her since he and Wendall had appeared at the gate to check on her welfare? So many hours had passed since then. It was possible they were already too late. He couldn't dwell on that. The idea that she might be hurt—or worse—would destroy him.

He moved like a shadow in the cold night, his feet skipping over the frozen earth without making a sound. Troy would head to the left side of the house, Micah to the right and Lucas would take the rear. Somehow they would get inside. It was what they were trained to do.

With every step he took he saw her again and again, tugging on that golden strand of hair, her lips curved into a pleasant smile as she'd lied to him and told him she was where she wanted to be.

Be safe, Julie. His heart thundered the words, and it was in those moments as he ran toward the house, as his heart beat the frantic rhythm of fear, that he was struck again by the depth of his love for her.

She was the woman he'd want in his life if he were the man he wanted to be instead of the man he feared he was. Hopefully he could rescue her, get her to safety and then love her enough to let her go.

The moon cooperated with the mission, hiding its light behind a thick layer of clouds, and as Lucas approached the dark, quiet house, his heartbeat slowed and his anxiety level dropped.

He called it mission mode, when all thoughts left his head and he was filled with a cold calm. All emotion fell away, replaced by the steely determination of a soldier.

There wasn't a single light on anywhere in the house that could be seen, and yet even with the hidden moon overhead there was a faint illumination.

Where are you, Julie? They all had agreed that she was probably being held on the second or third floor.

He reached the side of the house and looked up, but there was no clue as to which of the dozens of windows she might be behind.

A faint crunch of icy grass came from the side of the house. Lucas flattened himself with his back against the building just as the dark outline of a tall, thin man came into view.

A guard, Lucas quickly surmised. He walked at a leisurely pace, letting Lucas know he had no clue that their security had been breached.

Still, Lucas knew his safest course of action was to take the man out. He narrowed his gaze as the guard drew closer, making a wide circle around the back of the house.

If he saw Lucas, then he might get an opportunity to alert others before Lucas could neutralize him. Lucas stopped breathing, hoping, praying he wouldn't be seen.

Crouching for attack, he waited until the man had his back to him; then he sprang.

It took less than five seconds to get the man in a sleeper hold and render him unconscious. As he fell to the ground, Lucas quickly taped his mouth closed and tied his hands and legs, then dragged him away from the house and into the field beyond.

Moments later he sprinted back and once again eyed the house. *Now to find a way inside,* he thought. His mission-mode calm slipped away as he thought of Julie, and prayed that they would get to her in time.

JULIE LAY IN BED in the darkened room, sleep the furthest thing from her mind. Tonight was her last night on earth.

Robert had told her when he'd left her room earlier that tomorrow she would be undergoing a cesarean section. She knew that they would take her baby and she would die. There was no way they could allow her to live. She was a loose end, a liability in their crazy plan.

She closed her eyes and rubbed her tummy. Robert would raise her son as his own, and groom him to usher a congregation from a good, religious group to a dangerous, powerful cult. When Robert had first told her his plan, she'd asked why it had to be her baby. He'd told her it was the bloodline that mattered. If anyone in the congregation questioned that the child wasn't of his own bloodline then he'd have DNA proof. He'd promised his congregation a child of his blood, and a nephew would fit the bill just fine.

With the hours that she'd had to think, she'd realized that it was possible that Robert had killed his brother, her husband.

Robert had known Julie was leaving David and that she'd just discovered she was pregnant at the time of David's death. It was possible he'd feared that she'd leave David and disappear into another life with her son. And Robert wanted her child.

If what she believed was true, then Robert had taken a gamble. He'd wanted a child of his blood to fill the position of the son he'd never had. Julie and David's baby fit the bill. Still, if he'd killed David and she'd miscarried, he would never have gained the child he desperately wanted—needed—to complete his plan.

None of that mattered now. It was over. Robert was going to succeed and she was going to die. At least her regrets were few.

Although the pain of knowing she would never see her son, never hold his sweetness in her arms and watch him grow into a man, was too hard to bear, in every other area of her life there weren't many things she regretted.

She'd loved.

A vision of Lucas filled her head. With all her memories now intact she knew that what she'd felt for him hadn't been just gratitude. She loved him with a sweeping depth that she'd never felt for the man she'd married.

And she'd been loved.

She didn't care what Lucas said, he had loved her, too. Unfortunately his love for her hadn't been strong enough.

She knew it had to do with his father, with the miserable childhood he'd suffered. There was no way a child could go through that kind of experience and not be changed at the very core.

If only he could see himself through her eyes and embrace the man he was, a loving, giving man who might have made her life complete.

Her only regret was that she and Lucas had never gotten the chance to make love for real. She would never feel his hips against her own, the weight of his body on hers as he buried himself deep inside her.

Too late now.

She closed her eyes, begging for sleep to come and take her away from her thoughts. She had almost drifted off when a faint thud sounded just outside her door.

She shot up to a sitting position, her heart thundering alarm. What was that? Were they coming for her? Had they decided to take the baby now, tonight?

Her weary acceptance of what was to come disappeared as an unexpected adrenaline filled her. At that moment she realized she did not intend to go easy.

She would scratch and claw and fight whoever came inside to take her baby. She would kick and gouge and scream bloody murder even if it didn't help. She'd make sure she hurt them before they killed her.

She slid out of bed and grabbed the bedside lamp. With a single pull she yanked the cord from the plug in the wall. It was a tiny thing, by no means a lethal weapon, but she crept to the door and held it up over her head.

Her arms shook and her heart pounded so hard she felt half breathless as she waited to see if anyone would enter. Seconds ticked by and she began to think that maybe she'd imagined the noise she'd heard in the hallway.

She froze as she heard the scrape of a key in the lock, then the squeak of the knob slowly turning. As the door creaked open she tightened her hands on the base of the lamp.

As the dark figure stepped into the room, she crashed the lamp down on him, crying out in frustration as she realized she'd missed his head and hit him on his shoulder.

He whirled around and grabbed her by the shoulders, his big, strong fingers biting painfully tight into her tender flesh. She screamed and was instantly backhanded with a slap that nearly sent her to her knees.

"Shut up," Robert said. "If you scream again I'll

knock you unconscious." He batted the lamp out of her hand and grabbed her. "Let's go. We're moving out of here. Security has been breached."

He jerked her out into the dim hallway, where only faint night-lights lit the area. It was like her dream, the long hallway and the eerie lighting. Only this time she wasn't running alone, she was being dragged by the man who wanted her dead.

It was only as they stepped out of the bedroom that she realized he had a gun, and her heart once again knocked so hard against her ribs it nearly took her breath away. "If you make a sound, I'll put a bullet in your brain," he whispered as he pulled her up against him.

What was happening? Why was he moving her out of her bedroom in the middle of the night? And why was he doing it at gunpoint?

They moved slowly, passing dark rooms with open doors. Where was he taking her? It was obvious he was moving in the direction of the back staircase that would eventually take them into the kitchen of the large house. In the kitchen was a door that led to the garage.

Was he moving her completely out of the house? Was he taking her someplace where a doctor awaited to cut her baby from her and toss her dead body on some deserted city street?

She might have fallen to the floor in utter despair if they hadn't passed another room. As she glanced inside she could have sworn she saw the movement of a dark, silent shadow just inside the door.

Her heart skipped a beat and a tiny flicker of hope ignited inside her. Lucas? Her heart cried his name. Was it possible he had caught her attempt to signal him when she'd pulled on the end of her hair?

Had he realized she'd been lying to him when she'd told him everything was all right? Or had she simply imagined that dark form in the room because she desperately wanted to be rescued? Or had the dark shadow simply been one of Robert's henchmen?

Closer and closer they got to the stairs that would lead them down and out of the house. Knowing that if he managed to get her outside, nobody would ever know what had become of her, she dragged her feet, making it difficult for them to make forward progress.

When they passed another dark room and she thought she saw the shadowy figure of a man, she wondered if she was losing her mind, if the stress of the situation had her seeing phantoms.

She never heard them coming. The phantoms seemed to jump out of the very woodwork, two behind them and one in front of them, blocking their way down the hall.

She also didn't see the blow that sent the gun flying from Robert's hand. Everything happened in a blur. One of the shadows grabbed her, and the minute she was pulled against his chest she knew it was Lucas.

Tears sprang to her eyes, and she might have wept with relief if it wasn't for the sound of running footsteps coming from the opposite end of the hallway.

Lucas shoved her behind him and turned to face the next challenge. Somebody turned on the hall lights, and as Julie cowered against the wall, her hands protectively splayed across her belly, all hell broke loose.

Lucas and his partners faced off against Robert and the two other men who had appeared in the hallway. As Robert dove for the gun he had dropped, Lucas jumped on his back while Troy and Micah began hand-to-hand combat with the others.

"Take her and go," Micah yelled as he rendered his opponent unconscious, then jumped on Robert's back.

Lucas rose, his features set in grim lines as he grabbed Julie by the hand and pulled her toward the stairs. They raced downward as fast as she was capable of going. They wouldn't be safe until they were out of this house, away from this compound.

Down the two flights of stairs they flew, and when they reached the kitchen they burst out the back door. Julie hadn't realized she was crying until the cold air slapped her wet cheeks.

"Wait," she said, and stopped in her tracks. Even though she knew they needed to get out of there as quickly as possibly, the run down the stairs had winded her. She bent over slightly and drew in deep gulps of air.

She gasped in surprise as Lucas scooped her up in his arms and continued across the field toward the high fence in the distance. She buried her head in his shoulder, awed by his strength, by the chance he had taken to come in to get her.

It was only when they reached the fencing that he set her back on her feet. Troy and Micah grinned at them from the other side of the fence. "What took you so long?" Micah asked, and pulled apart a section of the steel links that had been cut away.

"I stopped to smell the roses," Lucas replied drily. Julie stepped through the hole in the fence and Lucas followed.

"I'm taking her right to the police station," Lucas said. "I suggest you two lie low until we see how this all plays out. Any casualties?"

"Nothing that a little time and a few bandages won't heal," Troy replied.

"Call Wendall and tell him to meet me at the station," Lucas said to Troy, who nodded.

"Let's move," Micah added. The two men headed for their vehicles, and Lucas and Julie raced for his. Within minutes they were driving away from Julie's nightmare and Julie was telling him everything she remembered, everything that Robert had planned.

Lucas said nothing, he just listened until she was finished telling her story. By that time they were in front of the police station.

As he turned off the engine of his car she placed a hand on his arm. "Lucas, before we go inside, I need to tell you something," she said.

"What's that?" His gaze was enigmatic in the spill of light from the nearby police station.

"In the hours tonight as I contemplated my own death, the one thing that kept me strong was my love for you. Not gratitude, Lucas. Love. I love you, Lucas Washington, and if you look in your heart I know that you'll see that you love me, too."

"It doesn't matter what's in my heart," he said, his features looking starker, more sharp than usual as a pulse knotted in his jaw. "I told you from the start of this that I don't want a wife."

He started to open his car door, but she stopped him by grabbing his arm. "Is it because of the baby? You can't love a baby that isn't yours?"

"Of course not," he replied without hesitation. "I could love a baby—I could love your baby, but I told you I don't want to be a husband or a father."

"Why not? What are you afraid of, Lucas? Why would you deny yourself the joy of a woman who loves you? A family who could fill your life?"

"We don't have time for this," he said impatiently.

"That's one thing I realized as I was waiting to die," she exclaimed. "The only real thing we have time for on this earth is to love and to be loved."

He stiffened. "I will not repeat the mistakes of my father," he said in a voice that trembled with suppressed emotion.

"No, you won't," she agreed. "Because you are not anything like your father. Oh, Lucas, why can't you see yourself as I see you, as your sister sees you? How long will you allow the shadow of your father to keep all light from your heart?"

A headlight beam from an arriving car bathed Lucas's face in stark brightness. "That's Wendall. Let's go inside." Before she could stop him he opened his door and got out of the car.

For the next several hours Julie sat with Chief Kincaid and a prosecuting attorney in an interrogation room where she told them everything that had happened from the time of her husband's murder to the present. She now knew why she had been so terrified of coming to the police, and she told Wendall of Officer Ben Branigan's involvement with Robert's plans.

Lucas had disappeared. She assumed he was being questioned in another room. Several times Wendell left and was gone for long minutes only to return for more questioning.

She was completely wrung out by the time Wendall called a halt to things. "I've arranged a room for you at a nearby hotel for the next couple of days," he said. "You'll be under guard until we can sort all this out."

He smiled for the first time since they'd begun the questioning process. "Don't worry, Julie. We'll make sure you and your unborn baby are safe now."

She nodded wearily. "Can I see Lucas now?"

He looked surprised. "Lucas left here some time ago. He told me to tell you goodbye for him. Now, let's get you settled in for the night."

Numb. She was numb as Wendall escorted her from the room and introduced her to Officer Clay

Samuels, who would be taking her to her hotel and standing guard for the next twelve hours.

He left without saying goodbye. He'd made sure she was safe, he'd listened to her tell him that she loved him, but ultimately he'd made the choice to walk away from her. She had a horrible feeling that she would never hear from, never see him again.

Chapter Thirteen

"Want more coffee?" Loretta asked Lucas as she got up to pour herself another cup.

"No, thanks, I'm fine. What are your plans for the day?" he asked once she'd joined him at the table.

"I'm going shopping for a dress to wear to Micah's wedding," she replied. "And then I'm meeting Joe for lunch."

Joe was the coworker she'd had a date with, the coworker Lucas suspected might eventually become his brother-in-law. Even as she said his name her eyes took on a new sparkle.

"When do I get to meet this guy?" Lucas asked with a touch of impatience.

"I don't know—not yet. We'll see how things go in the next couple of weeks," she replied with a smile. "What do you have planned for the day?"

Lucas glanced out the window, where it was yet another cold, gray day. "I'm not sure. I'm kind of at loose ends." For the last week he, Micah and Troy had kept a low profile, not even going into the Recovery Inc. offices as they waited for the dust to settle following their raid on the Church of Enlightenment compound. The D.A. had decided not to press any charges against the men who had rescued Julie.

"I heard they made some more arrests yesterday," Loretta said, as if she knew his thoughts.

He nodded and focused back on her. "That makes fourteen. I spoke to Wendall late last night and he told me he thought they'd arrested everyone that had anything to do with Julie's case."

"And they'll all be charged with kidnapping?"

"Among other charges." He picked up his coffee cup and took a sip, trying not to think about Julie. He wasn't even sure where she was now, told himself it was enough just to know that she was safe.

According to what Wendall had told him the night before, they had recovered enough information off Robert's computer to see that he'd spend most of the rest of his life behind bars. He'd kept a diary, filled with plans and sermons he would give his congregation to welcome in the new little prophet.

It never failed to amaze Lucas how stupid criminals could be when it came to their computers and what they typed in, believing that they wouldn't get caught, that nobody would ever see their incriminating records.

They'd also managed to find the doctor who had been going to take the baby from Julie and allow her to die. Martha Montgomery had been a weak link, and according to Wendall, was spilling her guts in hopes of cutting a deal with the prosecution.

"Troy proposed to Brianna," he said, once again to get his mind off the thoughts of the woman who had haunted him for the last week.

"Good for him," Loretta replied. "Did they set a date for the wedding?"

"Not yet, although they're thinking sometime in the spring." And they all lived happily ever after. The words that ended every fairy tale flittered through his head.

Micah would soon make Caylee his bride, Troy and Brianna would follow and begin a family and eventually Loretta might marry her Joe.

"The only real thing we have time for on this earth is to love and to be loved." Julie's words whirled around in his head.

"You've invited them all for Thanksgiving dinner?" Loretta asked.

He nodded and stood abruptly. "I've got to get going," he said, needing to do something, anything that would keep him too busy to think. He carried his cup to the sink just as Loretta's phone rang.

She answered as he washed out his cup and put it in her dishwasher. By the time he turned to face her, she'd already hung up.

"That was Julie," she said. "She's in labor and on her way to the hospital." Loretta looked at him expectantly.

A rush of crazy emotions blew through him. *"You won't have that baby alone. I'll make sure of that."* Wasn't that what he'd told her? Wasn't that what he'd promised her?

It hadn't been a real promise, he tried to tell himself. It had just been a statement made in the heat of a moment.

As he stood there, frozen in place, Loretta's look of expectation turned to one of faint disgust. "You're a fool, Lucas. I know you love her and I know what's holding you back. In a million years, under a million circumstances, you could never be like him."

She grabbed her purse from the countertop. "You're my hero, Lucas. You always have been, but a hero isn't afraid of loving somebody. I'm going to the hospital, because Julie needs somebody with her. I'm not the person she really wants, but I guess I'll have to do."

She marched out of the kitchen without a backward glance, and a moment later Lucas heard the slam of her front door. He remained standing in the stillness of the kitchen, alone as he'd always been, alone as he should be.

JULIE FELT THE GRIP of another contraction coming on and tried to breathe slowly and evenly as she succumbed to the pain that would eventually usher in the birth of her son. She panted as the pain slowly eased away.

"Three minutes apart. It won't be long now," the

nurse said cheerfully. "You're doing just fine, Julie. I'm going to check in with the doctor. I'll be right back."

As she left the room Julie turned her head to look out the hospital room window. The gray, overcast skies could do nothing to detract from the joy of the knowledge that in a short period of time she'd have her baby boy in her arms.

The only thoughts that might have stolen a tiny bit of joy from her were of Lucas. She tried desperately to keep him out of her mind.

For the last five days while she'd been alone in her hotel room, Lucas was all she'd been able to think about. She'd almost wished she could call back her amnesia and forget everything that had happened from the moment he'd found her in the back of that car to when he'd walked out of the police station without a backward glance.

Unfortunately, selective amnesia didn't seem to be in her power, and thoughts of what might have been had haunted her throughout those days and nights.

With yesterday's arrests, Chief Kincaid had told her that he thought she was no longer in danger. Everyone she remembered being part of the plot to steal her baby was now in jail.

Last night she'd moved back into the house she'd shared with David. She would live there until it sold, then hopefully she'd have enough to cover a couple of months of living expenses. Next fall she intended to return to teaching.

The future was an open book filled with potential and all she had to do was stop thinking about a particular black-haired, dark-eyed man who had stolen her heart.

She'd called Loretta several times during the past week, finding solace in the friendship that the two had built in the brief time they'd spent together. In none of those conversations had Lucas's name come up.

As she felt another contraction beginning to build, she clenched her fingers into the sheets as tears blurred her vision. They weren't tears of pain, but rather ones of disappointment. She'd called Loretta, but she hadn't shown up yet.

I can do it alone, she told herself as a whimper escaped her lips. She knew she was strong, perhaps stronger than most women. She'd just endured an ordeal that few would ever experience and she'd come out of it okay.

She closed her eyes as the pain shot through her. Another whimper slipped from her mouth, this one a little bit louder. She was vaguely aware of somebody coming back into the room and suddenly her hand was clasped in a bigger, stronger one.

Her eyes flew open and she gasped as she saw Lucas, his dark eyes radiating with her pain. "Breathe, Julie," he said softly.

She closed her eyes as his hand squeezed hers tightly and she breathed, riding the wave of pain more easily just knowing he was with her.

When the contraction subsided, she looked at him once again. Was he here because Loretta had insisted he come? Because he'd made her a promise and Lucas was a man of his word?

She was afraid to hope for anything more. "I'm naming him Luke," she said with more than a touch of defiance. "And if you don't like it you can just lump it."

He raised a dark eyebrow with a teasing smile. "Lump it?"

"You know what I mean," she replied. "What are you doing here, Lucas?"

He pulled up a chair next to the side of her bed and sat, then once again took her hand in his. "Somebody very wise once told me that the only real thing we have time for on this earth is to love and to be loved."

Her heart skipped a beat as she eyed him cautiously. "That still doesn't answer my question."

The teasing smile that had curved his lips faltered and it was with complete seriousness that he gazed at her. "As crazy as it sounds, I think I fell more than half in love with you the minute I saw you in the back of that car. You knew I was in love with you. Loretta knew I was in love with you. Even I knew it. But you scare the hell out of me."

"You're an ex–navy SEAL. Nothing should scare you," she protested.

"Not being the man I want to be has always scared me," he replied.

"But you're the man *I* want you to be. You're the man I want in my life forever. Oh, Lucas, don't you see?" The last word rose an octave as a new contraction ripped through her.

It seemed to last forever and was followed by another one almost immediately. The doctor swept into the room and smiled at Lucas. "Ah, I see we're all here—mommy and daddy. And very soon we'll have little junior here with us."

Julie knew she should correct the doctor, tell him that Lucas wasn't the daddy, that he was just here because he'd made a stupid promise.

She should tell the doctor that Lucas would be here only long enough to see the birth of the baby and then he would disappear from her life once again.

But she couldn't tell him, she couldn't speak a single word as waves of pain tore through her. Lucas grabbed her hand, his eyes shining overly bright as the doctor got into position at the foot of her bed and told her to push.

"Push, Julie. Let's get this baby born," he said.

She bore down with a low scream as tears blurred her vision. The tears were a mix of pain and joy. *Come on, son,* she begged as she stopped bearing down and tried to catch her breath.

"You're doing great, Julie," Lucas said as he swept a strand of her damp hair away from her face.

"Again, Julie," the doctor said. "Push."

"Come on, honey, that little boy wants to be born," Lucas said. "Push."

She did. Over and over again she grunted and pushed to give birth.

"That's it," Lucas exclaimed. "You are so beautiful," he exclaimed as he swept her damp hair away from her forehead. "You're the bravest woman I know."

"I can't do it anymore," she exclaimed in exhaustion.

"Yes, you can," Lucas replied. "I love you, Julie, and I love that baby. Now, push!"

Although his words and actions of love were welcomed, in the back of her mind she knew not to embrace them into her heart. The ability to think fell away as she gave herself into the gripping pain of birth and the knowledge that this moment with Lucas wouldn't last forever.

NIGHT HAD FALLEN and outside her hospital window the sky was filled with stars. It was as if the clouds had parted to reveal the beautiful starlit night sky just for little Luke.

He lay in her arms, sleeping soundly, and snuggled against the reassuring sound of her heartbeat. Love swelled up inside her as she kissed the top of his little bald head.

She'd slept most of the afternoon, exhausted by the birth. A nurse had awakened her a little while ago and told her it was time to feed her boy.

The birth itself now felt like a dream, the memory of pain gone beneath the overwhelming joy. Had she dreamed of Lucas when in the throes of childbirth?

Immediately after little Luke had made his appearance, Lucas had done a vanishing act, and she hadn't seen him since. She really hadn't expected anything else. He'd fulfilled his promise that she wouldn't have the baby alone, and now he owed her nothing more.

"We're going to be just fine," she whispered to Luke. "We're going to have a wonderful life together."

Once again she turned her head to look out her window. No point in wishing on a star for a man who refused to make a commitment despite his pronouncements of love for her.

Instead, she wished for a long and happy life for her son, a world filled with laughter and love. She would give him that. She would give him all the love she had in her heart.

A sound from the doorway drew her attention. When she turned her head to see who was there, her breath caught in her chest.

Lucas stood just inside the room. In one hand he held a huge bouquet of flowers, and in the other arm he gripped the biggest teddy bear she'd ever seen.

"I didn't think I'd ever see you again," she said.

"Yeah, I didn't think you would, either." He placed the flower arrangement on a nearby table, the teddy bear in a chair and then moved to stand beside her bed.

In the dim lighting of the room his eyes glowed as he gazed at her. "I thought I could walk away from you—from him—but I can't. For the first time in my life, my love is bigger than my fear."

He sank down in the chair next to her, as if his legs wouldn't hold him up any longer. She didn't say a word, afraid that in doing so she might break the moment.

"I've done nothing but think about you since I left the police station a week ago. The last week has been the longest in my life, but I was determined to stay away from you. Then Loretta told me you were in labor and I knew this was where I needed, where I wanted to be."

He paused and reached for her hand. "I'm not my father and in a million years I could never be my father. I've wasted too many years of my life worrying about what I might become instead of recognizing the kind of man I am."

"I've been trying to tell you that," she finally said, her heart more full than it had ever been in her entire life.

He grinned sheepishly. "You should know by now that I'm hardheaded." His grin disappeared and he leaned forward, his eyes shining with a suspicious moisture. "I love you, Julie, and I want a life with you, with Luke. I want to be the man in both of your lives."

"Lucas Washington, if you don't kiss me this minute I think I might die," she exclaimed.

He grinned, that sexy smile that swelled her heart even bigger. He stood and bent over, capturing her lips in a kiss that flamed through her with a wealth of new promises.

When the kiss finally ended, he drew back from her and gently tucked a strand of her hair behind her ear. "You'll be home for Thanksgiving, Julie. You and Luke will be home with me."

As the stars twinkled outside the window, Julie felt the fire of a comet in her soul, but she knew it was nothing more than the sweet warmth of love.

* * * * *

Celebrate 60 years of pure
reading pleasure with Harlequin!

To commemorate the event, Harlequin
Intrigue® is thrilled to invite you to the
wedding of The Colby Agency's J. T. Baxley
and his bride, Eve Mattson.

That is, of course, if J.T. can find the woman
who left him at the altar. Considering he's a
private investigator for one of the top agencies
in the country—the best of the .best—that
shouldn't be a problem. The real setback is that
his bride isn't who she appears to be…and her
mysterious past has put them both in danger.

Enjoy an exclusive glimpse of
Debra Webb's latest addition to
THE COLBY AGENCY: ELITE
RECONNAISSANCE DIVISION

THE BRIDE'S SECRETS

Available August 2009 from Harlequin Intrigue®.

The dark figures on the dock were still firing. The bullets cutting through the surface of the water without the warning boom of shots told Eve they were using silencers.

That was to her benefit. Silencers decreased the accuracy of every shot and lessened the range.

She grabbed for the rocks. Scrambled through the darkness. Bumped her knee on a boulder. Cursed.

Burrowing into the waist-deep grass, she kept low and crawled forward. Faster. Pushed harder. Needed as much distance as possible.

Shots pinged on the rocks.

J.T. scrambled alongside her.

He was breathing hard.

They had to stay close to the ground until they reached the next row of warehouses. Even though she was relatively certain they were out of range at this point, she wasn't taking any risks. And she wasn't slowing down.

J.T. had to keep up.

The splat of a bullet hitting the ground next to Eve had her rolling left. Maybe they weren't completely out of range.

She bumped J.T. He grunted.

His injured arm. Dammit. She could apologize later.

Half a dozen more yards.

Almost in the clear.

As she reached the cover of the alley between the first two warehouses she tensed.

Silence.

No pings or splats.

She glanced back at the dock. Deserted.

Time to run.

Her car was parked another block down.

Pushing to her feet, she sprinted forward. The wet bag dragged at her shoulder. She ignored it.

By the time she reached the lot where her car was parked, she had dug the keys from her pocket and hit the fob. Six seconds later she was behind the wheel. She hit the ignition as J.T. collapsed into the passenger seat. Tires squealed as she spun out of the slot.

"What the hell did you do to me?"

From the corner of her eye she watched him shake his head in an attempt to clear it.

He would be pissed when she told him about the tranquilizer.

She'd needed him cooperative until she formulated a plan. A drug-induced state of unconsciousness had been the fastest and most efficient method to ensure his continued solidarity.

"I can't really talk right now." Eve weaved into the right lane as the street widened to four lanes. What she needed was traffic. It was Saturday night—shouldn't be that difficult to find as soon as they were out of the old warehouse district.

A glance in the rearview mirror warned that their unwanted company had caught up.

Sensing her tension, J.T. turned to peer over his left shoulder.

"I hope you have a plan B."

She shot him a look. "There's always plan G." Then she pulled the Glock out of her waistband.

Cutting the steering wheel left, she slid between two vehicles. Another veer to the right and she'd put several cars between hers and the enemy.

She was betting they wouldn't pull out the firepower in the open like this, but a girl could never be too sure when it came to an unknown enemy.

Deep blending was the way to go.

Two traffic lights ahead the marquis of a movie theater provided exactly the opportunity she was looking for.

The digital numbers on the dash indicated it was just past midnight. Perfect timing. The late movie would be purging its audience into the crowd of teenagers who liked hanging out in the parking lot.

She took a hard right onto the property that

sported a twelve-screen theater, numerous fast-food hot spots and a chain superstore. Speeding across the lot, she selected a lane of parking slots. Pulling in as close to the theater entrance as possible, she shut off the engine and reached for her door.

"Let's go."

Thankfully he didn't argue.

Rounding the hood of her car, she shoved the Glock into her bag, then wrapped her arm around J.T.'s and merged into the crowd.

With her free hand she finger-combed her long hair. It was soaked, as were her clothes. The kids she bumped into noticed, gave her death-ray glares.

They just didn't know.

As she and J.T. moved in closer to the building, she grabbed a baseball cap from an innocent by-stander. The crowd made it easy. The kid who owned the cap had made it even easier by stuffing the cap bill-first into his waistband at the small of his back.

Pushing through the loitering crowd, she made her way to the side of the building next to the main entrance. She pushed J.T. against the wall and dropped her bag to the ground. Peeled off her tee and let it fall.

His gaze instantly zeroed in on her breasts, where the cami she wore had glued to her skin like an extra layer. A zing of desire shot through her veins.

Not the time.

With a flick of her wrist she twisted her hair up and clamped the cap atop the blonde mass.

"They're coming," J.T. muttered as he gazed at some point beyond her.

"Yeah, I know." She planted her palms against the wall on either side of him and leaned in. "Keep your eyes open. Let me know when they're inside."

Then she planted her lips on his.

* * * * *

Will J.T. and Eve be caught in the moment?
Or will Eve get the chance to
reveal all of her secrets?
Find out in
THE BRIDE'S SECRETS
by Debra Webb
Available August 2009 from Harlequin Intrigue®